*"Don't," she m_____
presume to kno_____
Or what I feel,_____*

She'd read his thoughts; she knew his fear.
He nodded. "You're right. I don't have a
gift, not like you." But he was cursed all
the same.

Placing her slim hands on his shoulders,
she pushed him down so he sat on the edge
of the rusted tub. Then she ran her fingers
through his hair and over his scalp. He
didn't notice the pain, only the heat of her
touch. Like her kiss, it branded him.

Sucking her bottom lip between her teeth,
she murmured, "You have a few deep cuts.
You could probably use some stitches. Let
me clean them, at least."

"Irina…"

"You've asked me to trust you. You need
to trust me."

More than once he'd requested her trust,
and she'd given it. Trust didn't come as
easily for Ty.

"You think it comes easy for me?" she
asked. "I don't even trust myself."

Dear Reader,

Damned is the conclusion of my WITCH HUNT trilogy for NOCTURNE. I've loved writing about all the "gifted" Cooper sisters, but I couldn't wait to tell Irina's story, partly because, as the youngest of my family, I can identify with her, but mostly because *Damned* is also Ty McIntyre's story. The witch hunt has put Ty through a lot of physical and emotional trauma. He's lost his job and a chance with the woman he thought he could love. He deserves to find the true love of his life, and he deserves to make sure justice is finally served. I hope you enjoy reading Ty and Irina's story as much as I enjoyed writing it!

Happy reading!

Lisa

Damned
LISA CHILDS

MILLS & BOON®
Pure reading pleasure™

All the characters in this book have no existence outside the
imagination of the author, and have no relation whatsoever to anyone
bearing the same name or names. They are not even distantly inspired
by any individual known or unknown to the author, and all the
incidents are pure invention.

First published in Great Britain 2008
by Harlequin Mills & Boon Limited,
Eton House, 18-24 Paradise Road, Richmond, Surrey TW9 1SR

ISBN: 978 0 263 85998 0

46-1008

Harlequin Mills & Boon policy is to use papers that are
natural, renewable and recyclable products and made from
wood grown in sustainable forests. The logging and
manufacturing processes conform to the legal environmental
regulations of the country of origin.

Printed and bound in Spain
by Litografia Rosés S.A., Barcelona

ABOUT THE AUTHOR

Award-winning author Lisa Childs wrote her first book when she was six, a biography...of the family dog. Now she writes romantic suspense, paranormal romance and women's fiction. The youngest of seven siblings, she holds family very dear in real life and in her fiction, often infusing her books with compelling family dynamics. She lives in west Michigan with her husband, two daughters and a twenty-pound Siamese cat. For the latest on Lisa's spine-tingling suspense and heartwarming women's fiction, check out her website at www.lisachilds.com. She loves hearing from readers, who can also reach her at PO Box 139, Marne, MI 49435, USA.

Acknowledgement

To the Grand Rapids Police Department, thank you for allowing me to participate in the Citizens Police Academy, and thank you most of all for your selfless service to our city.

Dedication

To my family, for your constant love and support!

Prologue

This was home: the street. Where she slept. Where she ate—if she remembered to eat. Where she drank—if she could scrounge up enough money for a bottle. And the drugs—they were easier to score.

But even here she couldn't hide from the voices, couldn't drown them out. They kept whispering…in her head, the voices echoing in her mind. And it didn't matter…what she did.

She couldn't shut them out.

Cardboard shifted and crumpled beneath her as she curled into a ball against the wall of a brick building. The stench of moldy food and dirty diapers drifted from the Dumpster behind which she lay, but she hardly noticed. She hardly noticed anything…outside her head.

She pressed her hands against her ears, trying to block out the noise. Not the rumble of traffic from the street, nor the murmured conversation drifting from the other end of the alley where shadows crouched around a barrel with flames lapping up the rusted rim.

The noise she tried to block was already inside her head, and her efforts were futile. As the voices rose, her vision dimmed, the stars, the street lamps and the fire at the end of the alley reduced to sparks in a sea of black. Blinded, her hearing sharpened.

"Where could Irina be?"

The sparks glittered and danced against the black backdrop as she struggled to recognize the voice.

"We have to find her before *he* does!"

Although she didn't think she'd ever heard either of the two soft feminine voices before, in person, they were oddly familiar. Despite the anxiety in these adult voices, each of them resonated with the echo of a child's laughter.

Her sisters…

She'd had sisters, hadn't she? Her parents had

told her no, that she'd been an only child. That she was only theirs. But there was another life to which she belonged…and it was calling her back.

"Irina…"

"Irina!"

She'd once been called Irina, twenty years ago, before she'd been taken away from her mother and her sisters. Before she'd been adopted by a couple who had wanted her to forget who she'd once been. They'd tried to convince her that she'd been born to them, that she'd been born Heather Bowers. But they hadn't adopted her until she was nearly five. She remembered. And even if she hadn't, she'd heard their thoughts; she knew the truth.

She wasn't theirs, and because of her uncanny ability to read their minds, they didn't want her to be. They couldn't love her. But they'd tried.

The way her sisters were trying to find her now. Why after all these years?

The sparks brightened like embers on a stoked fire as the voices quavered with fear.

"If he finds her first, he'll kill her like he killed the others."

"Like he killed *our* mother."

She squeezed her eyes shut so that even the sparks of light disappeared. But she couldn't shut out the voices. Others called to her, jumbled inside her head, echoes of thoughts and fears she'd already heard.

"I'm not a witch."

"Don't kill me! Please, don't kill me!"

But the killer ignored their pleas, and the women's voices rose in screams of terror and pain. Irina winced at the volume, which threatened to shatter her skull, and she cringed at the agony expressed in each shrill cry. No matter how long ago she'd first heard them, she couldn't get them out of her head, couldn't forget their suffering. Not only had she heard their cries but she'd felt their pain, too. The fire scorching her flesh, burning her alive. The noose chafing her skin, tightening around her throat until it cut off her last breath. The jagged rocks piled one by one onto her body, crushing her beneath their weight.

She'd wanted to help them, but she hadn't known where the women were. She hadn't been able to see them or their surroundings; she'd only heard them. Even if she had been able to figure out where they'd been, she would have been too late to save them. She'd wanted to help, but she couldn't even help herself right now.

One of these screams, the first she'd heard filled with such agony and fear and so hauntingly familiar, had driven her back here…to the street. Her biological mother's. She hadn't heard her voice in twenty years—not in person, just many times inside her head. With that scream she'd known her mother had been killed even before she'd heard her sisters speak of her death.

Were they real? Any of them? The voices? Her memories? Or had that first scream been the beginning of some kind of psychotic break?

Before hearing that scream, just months ago, she'd been managing. She'd been living. Going to school. Working.

Now she was barely existing, just waiting…until the next scream…was hers.

Chapter 1

Were they witches? They didn't cast spells. They didn't heal with potions and herbs as their long-dead ancestor had. But they had special abilities and they needed to use them to save a life—just as their ancestor had tried three hundred and fifty years ago. He only hoped their efforts weren't rewarded the same way hers had been.

With death.

Ty McIntyre cared about these two women. They sat together, holding hands, on the black leather couch in the penthouse owned by Ty's best friend. Actually Ariel held her older sister's hand,

and Elena held the charms—a little pewter sun and a little pewter star—in her palm, combining their powers.

Their powers?

A muscle jumped in his cheek as he clenched his jaw. Skepticism nagged at him. God, he was a lawman. Even though he *listened* to his instincts, he *relied* on evidence. Tangible proof. How could he rely on something he didn't understand, something he couldn't trust?

Believe, he silently chanted to quell his doubts. He'd seen the proof of their powers in the results they wrought. Ariel was alive. Stacia, Elena's daughter, was alive. Because of their intangible powers.

"Can you see anything yet?" he asked Elena, frustration thickening his voice.

She scrunched shut her pale eyes, and her forehead furrowed with concentration. The knuckles on the hand holding the charms tightened and turned white, while her fingers reddened.

"She can't force her visions," Ariel defended her sister as she stared up at him through narrowed eyes. "What's up with you, Ty? You're edgier than usual. Did you find out something you haven't shared yet?"

He shook his head, then started pacing the marble floor of David's living room. Like a jolt from an electrical outlet, pain traveled up his leg from his not-quite-healed wound. Maybe the doctors were right—maybe he'd had them remove the cast too soon. "No, I haven't learned a damned thing."

"So that's why you're edgy," Ariel said. "You're frustrated."

"We all are," Elena chimed in, her eyes still closed. "Since we know who the killer is, we should be able to find him."

Donovan Roarke. The man was a private investigator, but before that he'd been a cop. Like Ty. And like Ty, he'd been suspended from the police department due to excessive force. Ty's guts knotted, but he reminded himself he was nothing like the madman. Donovan Roarke was a sadistic son of a bitch. He might have convinced himself that by killing witches in the ways that witches had been killed centuries ago he was honoring his family legacy, the vendetta begun so many years ago. But Ty knew the guy was a psychopath, and if he wasn't caught soon, he'd kill again.

Anger gripped Ty, but he fought it off, breathing slow and deep. Then he shoved a hand through his hair. Even though he hadn't worn his uniform in months, he kept his black hair short, in an almost military cut. He liked his life simple, like the T-shirts and old jeans he wore. But there was nothing simple about his life now; there hadn't been since Donovan Roarke had begun his witch hunt.

"Roarke's clever," Ty admitted. Or he would have found the sick bastard by now.

"He's crazy," Ariel maintained.

Maybe Ty was, too, because he'd actually thought this might work, that Elena would have a vision that would lead him to her missing sister, the youngest of the three of them. Since he'd come up empty in his other investigations, he'd decided to use the sisters' powers. He had nothing left to lose.

"Let's concentrate on Irina," he said, which was easy for him since she was all he thought about lately.

She'd been nagging at his mind ever since he'd first seen the picture of her as a little girl. From the glass-and-marble coffee table he picked up the trifold pewter picture frame they'd found in Roarke's office. The private investigator must have stolen the twenty-year-old portraits of the three sisters from their mother after he'd killed her.

As Ty focused on the youngest child with her loose brown curls and her big, dark eyes, a memory teased him: flashing lights, blurred before his swollen eyes; pain pounding in his skull and tearing at his arm as he fought for consciousness, for life; then a little girl's voice calling out to him, calling him back from the brink of death.

Hers? Or the little girl who'd died because he hadn't gotten to her in time? Was the memory an old one, buried deep with the rest of his childhood? Or was it a new one, suppressed like the rage over which his lieutenant had suspended him?

His hand shaking slightly, he set the picture frame back on the table, then turned his attention to Elena. He'd deal with his own demons later, after he'd dealt with theirs. "You've had visions of her before. If you can't have another, try to remember everything you can about those, even what you might think insignificant."

Elena nodded in perfect understanding of the gift she'd denied and fought for so long. "I'll try to recall every detail."

He blew out a ragged breath, relieved that she understood what he wanted. Irina. "We have to find her." Soon.

Knowing who the killer was didn't make him less dangerous. In Roarke's case, Ty suspected knowing who he was made him *more* dangerous. Now the man wasn't worried about concealing his identity; he, like Ty, had nothing to lose.

Having tried and failed to get Ariel and Elena,

he'd concentrate all his efforts on Irina. And Ty would do the same. The others could look for Roarke; his friend David and Elena's fiancé Joseph were out now, searching for him. Ty already knew where he was—wherever Irina was.

"In that first vision you had of her, she's homeless." God, he hoped Elena was wrong, but he'd investigated the lead, spending days and nights among the street people. While he hadn't found Irina, he had found desperation and despair, reawakening memories he'd locked away in his past.

Elena shook her head. "I'm not even sure it's Irina I'm seeing. I haven't seen her since she was four."

"She was almost five," Ariel added, her turquoise eyes glistening with unshed tears. As if a year would have made a difference then.

Ariel had been nine, Elena twelve when they were taken away from their mother and separated from each other. Ty's gut twisted at having to bring up bad memories for them both. But the pain and fear they felt now would be worth it if he were able to reunite the sisters.

Ignoring the ache in his leg, he knelt on the floor in front of the couch, the marble cold through the denim of his faded jeans. Excessive force hadn't been his biggest hurdle in being a police officer; until his last day of active duty, he'd never had a problem dealing with suspects. His struggle had been dealing with the victims. Offering comfort—something never offered to him—hadn't been easy for him.

Now he reached out, closing his hand over their joined hands. "We'll find her."

Ariel stared into his eyes, hers still shimmering with tears. "Or will I, Ty? Will the first time I see my baby sister in twenty years be as a ghost?" Like she'd first seen her mother when Myra Cooper had been killed several months ago.

That was Ariel's gift—seeing ghosts; Elena's gift was seeing the future. What was Irina's? The lights flashed again, digging up the memory, but he couldn't pull it out of his mind. Not yet. He had too many other things on it.

He swallowed hard, then reminded her, "But you haven't seen Irina's ghost. She has to be alive."

His breath trapped in his lungs until she nodded her head in agreement. He shared her fear that they might not find Irina in time; it kept him from sleeping, from eating, from doing anything but search for her. Even though he had begun his quest to find the missing sister as a favor for his best friend and Ariel, it had become more personal to him. *Irina* was more personal to him than a twenty-year-old picture in an old pewter frame.

A moan slipped through Elena's lips. Her pale eyes glazed, she stared not at the opulent living room of the penthouse or the view outside the floor-to-ceiling windows, Barrett, Michigan, aglow with lights in the black sky. She stared instead at whatever images played out inside her head.

"Tell us everything you're seeing," he prodded her, as he would have any witness.

"She's on the street, like I saw her before," Elena said, taunted by the old vision like the old memory that wouldn't quite leave Ty alone.

"What do you see?" He needed some landmarks, something so he could pinpoint the place instead of wandering the streets the way he had.

"It's dark…."

"No street lamps?"

She squeezed her eyes closed, then shook her head. "Not here. The buildings are too tall. They block the light. So does the Dumpster."

"Then it's not a street. It's an alley." And he'd searched most of those in Barrett. But just because Irina had been adopted in Barrett didn't mean she still lived in the city, so he'd searched some surrounding areas, too. His gut twisted again at the thought of Irina in any of those dangerous areas, alone. "Tell me about the buildings. Describe them to me."

Elena's brow furrowed. "It's dark. All I see are walls of dark brick, maybe red, maybe brown—"

"A sign. Something—"

"Just the Dumpster. The name of the company's worn off the side. She's hiding behind the Dumpster."

Had she been in one of those alleys he'd searched, hiding? Had he been that close to finding her, to protecting her from a killer?

Come on, Irina. Come out. Stop hiding. Let me find you. Let me save you.

As she'd saved him? He shook his head, amazed that the thought had occurred to him, all wrapped up with the old, nagging memory. But looking into *his* past wouldn't help him find Irina; only looking into *her* future would.

"You have to concentrate. Focus on what's around her!" His agitation raised his voice above the usual rasp of his damaged vocal cords.

"Ty…" Ariel warned.

He expected Elena to protest, too, to remind him that her gift didn't work this way, on demand, as if she directed a camera onto a scene she'd orchestrated.

Her breath audibly caught, and she flinched at

whatever scene played out inside her head. This wasn't just a memory; she was in the midst of a vision. "Oh my God…"

"What?" he asked, his guts twisting again.

"She—she steps out from behind the Dumpster, she drags herself out of there. But it's too late." Her voice rose with a hint of hysteria. "She tries to run, but he catches her. He grabs her so hard. He's hurting her! She's too weak to fight him…too weak to save herself…."

Damn Donovan Roarke to hell! As soon as Ty tracked him down, he intended to send him there.

"It's okay," Ariel said, wrapping her arm around Elena's thin shoulders. "Your visions are of the future. This hasn't happened yet."

"But—"

"It hasn't happened yet," Ariel insisted.

"And it won't," Ty maintained. He wouldn't let Roarke get to Irina.

Maybe as desperate to convince herself as her sister, Ariel said, "He doesn't have her."

Yet.

"I've had this vision twice now," Elena reminded them, her voice cracking with emotion, her pale eyes shimmering with unshed tears and fear. "He's going to find her before we do. And we all know what he's going to do to her."

Kill her.

She had had that vision, too. The one of Irina dying just as horrifically as their mother had. Elena had gotten good at recounting her visions, but she had yet to find a way to deal with what she saw. She was shaking.

And so was Ty.

As Ariel had said, Elena's visions were of the future. Donovan didn't have her yet, but Ty suspected the madman was closer to finding her than Ty was. He had to beat the killer to her, because once Roarke got his hands on Irina, Ty would be too late to save someone. Again.

A new voice echoed in her head now, louder than all the others she'd heard before. And full of hatred. He talked about killing people, about making them suffer.

Irina knew about suffering, and lately not even the drugs or alcohol could relieve hers. She'd been weeks without and felt no different sober from inebriated. Except for the shaking. She couldn't stop shaking.

Summer had fled quickly from western Michigan, leaving early autumn cold, the nights chilly enough that she lost feeling in her fingers and toes. She might have to find someplace warmer than the alley to sleep. But then she'd have to deal with people.

Fear gripped her. Fear of the man inside her head. Because even though he hadn't said her name, like the women who called for her, she knew he intended to kill her as he had the other witches. He thought she was a witch and he wanted the charms he thought her mother had given her and her sisters two decades ago. He believed they were powerful, that they would heal the pain that reverberated inside his head.

And hers. She winced, pressing her palms against her eyes, blinded from the voices and the pain. Like the women he'd killed, she felt his torment as acutely as theirs. The hammering at the base of her skull and her temples. Her body reeled from the onslaught, and she writhed in agony on her makeshift bed behind the Dumpster.

She had to deal with the pain the best she could. She had to let go of reality and slip into the abyss, into the calm where her mind and spirit left her tortured body, where she ceased to exist as she had these past months.

But as she started slipping away, a raspy voice called out to her. "Irina…"

She moaned and shifted again on the bed, drawing her knees to her chest to curl into a ball.

She resisted the compulsion to open her eyes, refusing to come back into a world where she knew only pain and suffering.

"Irina, come out…."

But he was just as stubborn, refusing to let her go. She heard the determination in his voice, along with a trace of desperation. She recognized that more readily, as it called to her own.

"Irina, let me save you…."

His raspy whisper raised goose bumps on her skin. Was he nearby? Or even closer, inside her head?

She opened her eyes and blinked, clearing the sparks and the sea of black from her vision. All that loomed before her was the big Dumpster, the distant glow of the street lamps glinting off the rusted metal.

The cold reduced the stench, so only a faint odor of coffee grounds and mold drifted from it. But her stomach churned even though it was empty of everything but nerves. What had she done to herself? What had she become?

God, she'd been desperate for so long, desperate for a peace of mind she would probably never know.

"Irina, we need you…." called out a feminine voice, cracking with emotion. "We need our baby sister."

Another woman added her thoughts. "The

only way we can stop the witch hunt is with all three charms…."

Charms?

She peered up at the sky, at the sliver of crescent moon that hung high above the buildings, high above the earth. Out of Irina's reach, like the memory from her childhood of her sisters, of her mother…that last time she'd seen them before their family had been ripped apart. Pain and fear were all she remembered as she trembled under the renewed force of those emotions. She'd only been five then and she'd survived. She hadn't given up.

Until now…

Tears stung her eyes, tears of shame blinding her, but she could still see the alley. She could still see the bedraggled mess she had become…because she'd stopped fighting. Those other women—they hadn't given up. They'd fought for their lives, and two of them had survived and had saved those they cared about, one of them a little girl. Her cries had haunted Irina as much as her mother's. But the little girl had been brave, far braver than Irina.

Hadn't they survived? Or had she only imagined their courage? Either way, she envied it and had to emulate it if she were to survive, too.

She had to get out of the alley, get something to eat, a safe place to sleep—get her life back while she still had it. The drugs she'd taken had been prescription ones—some painkillers, some for schizophrenia—but even those hadn't stopped the voices. Maybe it was time she accepted that they were real. But if the voices were real, so was the killer. Dare she leave the alley? Dare she trust anyone?

"Believe," the raspy-voiced man murmured. But was he speaking to her or himself? What did he want to believe? Who was he? He'd called her name, as her sisters had. He wanted to find her, too. Why? For them or for himself?

She closed her eyes, sparks of deep blue glowing against the insides of her lids. Instead of fighting his voice, she blew out a breath and immersed herself in his mind. He didn't say anything else. The blackness remained, thick and impenetrable, with undercurrents of barely suppressed anger.

This man was no different than the other—full of rage. A killer. He wasn't going to *save* her. She couldn't trust him.

Could she trust herself? Could she trust her sanity?

She had to; she couldn't go on as she had, barely

existing. She opened her eyes, then reached for the Dumpster. Her fingers clawed at the rusted metal as she sought handholds to pull herself up. Her knees shook, threatening to fold, but she locked them and stood. Physically she was weak, but emotionally she was stronger than she'd been in a long time.

Her sisters were looking for her but couldn't find her. So *she* had to find *them*. Urgency rushed through her veins. Like those other women, the ones who hadn't survived, they were in danger. She remembered her sisters' voices calling out with fear and pain. But they had fought for their lives; they hadn't died, like their mother. They were still alive.

And so was Irina.

For the first time in a long time, she realized that. All the pain she'd felt, it hadn't been hers. She was fine, just weak. She staggered toward the street, but before she could leave the alley behind, a dark shadow stepped in front of her. She shrank back toward the Dumpster, not because she thought the hulking man one of the homeless who lived on the streets as she did but because she knew he wasn't.

The pain in his head pounded in hers as he silently spoke to her. *Witch, you weren't easy to find.*

If only she'd stayed hidden a little longer…

She shouldn't have let that raspy voice call her out of hiding. She shouldn't have listened to him.

She glanced behind her, toward where flames licked up the sides of the barrel at the end of the alley. No one stood around it, as they did every other night, as they had earlier that night.

"Help me!" she called out, praying they would emerge from the shadows where she was certain they hid, frightened of the stranger. They had no reason to fear him, not as she did. "Help me!"

"Shh," the man murmured aloud. "I'm not going to hurt you."

"Liar," she yelled at him, her throat scratchy from disuse. "Liar!"

He lifted his hands palms up, holding them out to her. "I'm here to help you," he insisted. "Your family sent me to find you."

She didn't hear what he spoke aloud, though. She read his demented mind. *Now that I have you, I can get the rest of your family. I can get the other charms. Then I'll kill all the witches.*

"No!" she screamed as she continued retreating from him. Her back, beneath the heavy wool sweater she wore over a threadbare T-shirt, warmed as she neared the burning barrel. Sweat, from fear and the heat, dribbled down between her shoulder blades.

"Come with me, Irina," the man said, his voice soft and low as if soothing a frightened animal. "I'll bring you to your sisters."

Then I'll kill all of you! Hang the redhead. Drown the blonde. Crush her daughter. And you, since you're the spitting image of your mother, I'll have to burn you at the stake, just like I burned her.

"Killer!" she shrieked at him. "You're a killer!"

"Shh…" he said again, for the first time glancing uneasily around at the shadows bouncing off the walls of the buildings that flanked the alley. "I'm a private investigator. I told you—your family sent me."

"I can hear you," she said. "Not what you're saying but what you're thinking. I can *hear* you!"

His dark eyes gleamed eerily as he stared at her. "You can hear me?"

"I know what you did. I know what you intend to do," she insisted.

But she wasn't going to let him. She whirled around to the other side of the barrel, then kicked over the rusted metal cylinder. The barrel broke apart, and the flames leaped toward him.

Throwing his arms up over his face, he shrank back against the wall of one of the buildings. Cowering as the barrel rolled toward him, sparks flying, he screamed, "No!"

Taking advantage of his distraction and distance, she ran from the alley, the heels of her worn shoes pounding the asphalt and scattering tin cans and paper debris as she headed toward the street. Her long skirt tangled around her legs, slowing her frantic dash.

You witch! When I catch you, you'll suffer. She heard his thought first, then his ragged breathing as he chased her.

Propelled by fear, she didn't dare stop running when she reached the curb, so she hurled herself into traffic. Tires squealed, brake pads burning, but the driver didn't stop in time. The metal bumper glanced off her thigh, knocking her onto the asphalt.

He would get her now; she couldn't run anymore. As big hands reached for her, closing around her arms, she screamed, her throat straining, her voice rising with hysteria. "Don't kill me! I'm not a witch! I'm not a witch!"

Chapter 2

Irina tugged on her wrists, trying to free her hands. But the bindings held her tight, trapped. Panic pressed on her chest, and her lungs labored for breath.

"Let me go!" she shouted, her throat raw from screaming. Tears pooled in the corners of her eyes from the pain. "Let me go! He's going to kill me!"

But no one believed her. If they had, they wouldn't have brought her here. To a psychiatric ward. She'd been in one before, but she hadn't been strapped down to a bed as she was now. She'd been an intern, not an inpatient. Committed.

She couldn't blame them for not believing her. She struggled to believe herself. Could she really hear other people's thoughts? Was that possible?

Maybe her earlier fear that she was hallucinating was founded. Maybe she belonged here. She sagged back against the mattress, which wasn't much softer than the thin cardboard over asphalt where she'd spent so much of the past few months. Even though an IV dripped saline into her arm, rehydrating her, she weakened, her lids drifting closed. Some doctor or nurse had injected her earlier with a sedative, which must have finally taken effect. Although her muscles relaxed and she breathed easier, her anxiety didn't lessen.

She wished *she* still believed she was crazy, that she was making up the horror her life had become. But she'd already accepted her truth. And she knew her fate.

He'd be coming back for her.

The doorknob rattled, startling her into fighting against the restraints. She thrashed on the bed, the springs and metal frame creaking in protest of her frantic movements.

"Stop it! You're going to hurt yourself," a young woman cautioned as she entered the room.

"*He's* going to hurt me. He's going to kill me!"

Despite the sedative, Irina's voice rose as the panic pressed down on her chest, stealing her breath.

"You've been saying that since the police brought you here." The woman wore the same green scrubs as the nurses but with a white coat. She wasn't much older than Irina; she'd probably just begun her residency. Irina didn't remember talking to her before.

"How long ago was that?" she asked—when she'd run in front of the police car, when a concerned officer had lifted her from the asphalt. She'd pleaded with them to save her from the man who'd been chasing her. But they hadn't seen him; like the homeless people in the alley, he'd disappeared into the shadows. But Irina had still been able to hear his thoughts and had known he watched her. She'd screamed that at them, too, that she could read his mind, that she could read theirs. They thought she was crazy. And so they'd brought her here.

"Last night," the doctor answered her. "So, tell me, who is this man you're afraid of?"

"I don't know." She hadn't even noticed the passing of time. He'd claimed to be a private investigator hired by her sisters to find her. But she knew he'd been lying.

"What's *your* name?" the woman asked.

Irina. She hadn't been called that in twenty years, not aloud, but now, locked in a psychiatric ward, with voices in her head, she felt more like Irina Cooper than she ever had Heather Bowers.

Since Irina hadn't answered her, the pretty young doctor probed, "Don't you know your name?"

For the first time in a long time, Irina felt as if she did *really* know who she was. But with the witch hunt resurrected, she wasn't about to admit to being Irina Cooper.

"I want to help you," the woman insisted, her dark eyes earnest.

If not for the voices, Irina would have been her. She'd *been* in her last year of medical school, after having already completed her master's in psychology, when the first scream had torn through her mind and torn apart her world. "I wish you could…."

But if she told the psychiatrist everything, the young doctor would think her even crazier than she already did.

The woman's face flushed with pink color. "Someone's been asking about you. At least I'm pretty sure you're the woman he's looking for. Maybe he'll be able to help you remember who you are."

He already had. But he didn't intend to let her make any more memories. God, how had he found her so quickly? He must have followed the police car to the psychiatric hospital.

Irina strained against the bindings at her wrists, trying to vault out of the bed. "You can't let him in here! Don't let him near me! He's going to kill me!"

"Why do you say that?" the psychiatrist asked, her face tight with concern. "Has he hurt you?"

Irina shook her head, tumbling her hair around her shoulders. Citrus shampoo wafted from her curls. The minute she'd been brought in, they'd washed her. Maybe he wouldn't recognize her from the dirty street person she'd been. Maybe she could convince him she wasn't who he thought she was.

She wasn't a witch.

Drawing in an unsteady breath, she admitted, "He hasn't touched me." *Yet.* "But I know he's hurt other people. He's killed them."

The young doctor's mouth pulled down at the corners. "He probably has, but only in the line of duty. He's a police officer."

No wonder he'd found her so quickly. Even if she somehow managed to free herself and escape, he would track her down again. She had to convince him she wasn't Irina Cooper. If she couldn't, she was damned.

As the psychiatrist opened the door and stepped into the hall, Irina tested the restraints, tugging on her wrists. Desperation to free herself renewed her struggle, and the straps dug deep grooves into her skin.

"She doesn't want to see you," the young doctor, her voice soft with apology, told someone in the corridor.

Irina held her breath as she listened for his response. But she couldn't discern his words, only the low timbre of his raspy murmur. Through the partially opened door she watched the psychiatrist's face, which flushed pink as she gazed up at the man who stood just outside Irina's line of vision.

The woman shook her head, shifting her braid against her back. Her hair was dark and long, like Irina's. "I'm sorry," she told him. "I don't want to upset her any further."

Unable to see or hear him through the door, Irina closed her eyes and listened for his voice inside her head. But now, when she actually wanted her mind invaded with the thoughts of others, it remained empty. Instead of blackness rolling in, she squinted against the stark glare of the fluorescent lights as she opened her eyes again. What had they given her?

She struggled anew against the restraints, wanting to pull out the IV as badly as she wanted her freedom. She needed to hear the voices now; she needed to know what was going on if she had any hope of protecting herself.

"Send him in," she yelled as the last of her strength drained from her body. The sedative had worked on her muscles as well as her mind, relaxing them so much that she couldn't even form a fist now. But even weak, she could fight him…if she could read his mind. He wouldn't dare to try to kill her here, in the hospital. And she'd be able to identify him. Maybe if he got close to her again, as he had in the alley, she could test her power.

Not that she'd ever had to have someone close to read his or her mind. She had no idea where those women were that he'd killed, but she'd heard their every terrified thought throughout their last moments. She shivered; her struggles to free herself had knocked her blankets to the floor, and she wore only a thin cotton gown. But her reaction was more from fear than cold.

She drew in a deep breath, reminding herself that she'd decided back in the alley that she was through running. Of course, a short while after making that decision she had run out in the street and into the path of that police car. The police officers hadn't helped her. Since he was one of them, there was no way she could trust them. Or anyone else. She had to help herself.

"I w-want to s-see him," she called out, her words slurred from the effects of the sedative. She blinked hard, fighting against exhaustion to keep her eyes open.

The door creaked as the man wedged his wide shoulders through the jamb and stepped into Irina's room, which shrank with his entrance. Like his shoulders, his chest was wide and heavily muscled beneath his thin cotton T-shirt. But his size, which was more muscle than height since he hovered just under six feet, didn't overwhelm Irina. He'd actually seemed bigger in the alley.

His intensity, apparent in his tautly clenched jaw and the hard stare of his navy-blue eyes, over-whelmed Irina. She tore her gaze from his, turning her attention to the woman who accompanied him. The psychiatrist followed closely behind Irina's visitor, probably whispering instructions on how not to get her patient hysterical again.

The doctor didn't have to worry about what he *said* to her. His *thoughts* were more likely to upset Irina—if she could tap into them the way she had before.

"Is she the woman you're trying to find?" the psychiatrist asked.

The man brushed a hand through his short black hair, in which the fluorescent lights picked up glints nearly as blue as his eyes. Irina forced herself to meet his gaze, expecting the burning hatred that had scorched her in the alley. But her vision dimmed, his face disappearing into the blackness that enveloped her. Only little sparks of blue relieved the dark.

His voice a raspy whisper, he lied to the doctor. "No." But his mind called out to her. *Irina?*

Her heart lurched with the shock of recognition of another kind. This wasn't the man who'd chased her from the alley. He was the man who'd made her consider leaving it in the first place, calling her name, telling her to believe.

"Who are you?" she asked.

The psychiatrist answered for him, "This is Ty McIntyre, a police officer."

Suspended police officer. She heard his silent amendment to the doctor's claim. More than that, her stomach muscles tightened with the pain and pride that omission, even silent, cost him.

"You don't recognize him?" the psychiatrist asked Irina. "He isn't the man you claim is trying to kill you?"

Oh God, the bastard has already found her!

Fear raised goose bumps on Irina's skin, but was it *her* fear or *his?* Irina shook her head. "No."

He was not the man she'd claimed was trying to kill her, but that didn't mean he wasn't just as dangerous—or maybe even more dangerous. Her connection with him was so strong, his thoughts so compelling that she had risked leaving her hiding place of the past few months. With the killer, she had only his actions to fear; with this man, she had her own to fear. She struggled to break the connection between them, fighting her way out of the darkness.

Yet the connection remained. The anger tightening the muscles in his stomach twisted hers into knots. Tension radiated from him as he stared at her.

She shifted against the mattress, unnerved by his intent scrutiny and her own inexplicable reaction to it. Her pulse quickened, her breath grew shallow and heat licked at her stomach.

The young psychiatrist cleared her throat. "Well, then…" she prompted the man as she pulled open the door again. "Since she isn't who you're looking for…"

"Who is she?" he asked as if Irina weren't in the room, as if he weren't staring directly into her eyes.

Irina lifted her chin, pride stinging at the way he'd dismissed her. But at least her pride had returned; she'd buried it for a long time under months of dirt and delusions. The voices hadn't been the delusion. Thinking herself crazy had been the delusion.

"Jane Doe, for now," the woman answered Ty McIntyre. "Until we learn her true identity."

Irina opened her mouth to tell him not the name she'd been given at birth but the one she'd been called the past twenty years. That was her legal identity but not her true one. But his anger coursed through her veins, burning her with its intensity. She didn't dare trust him. Too many people had died already. She didn't want anyone else to get hurt.

The faint echoes of old screams reverberated inside her head. She closed her eyes, refusing to relive the gruesome memories.

"Jane Doe," McIntyre repeated in a murmur, but in her mind, he shouted, *Irina Cooper. Irina Cooper.*

Since he knew who she was, why didn't he tell the psychiatrist? He must have a reason for keeping her identity secret. Irina wished she could read his intentions toward her in his thoughts. But she couldn't, and fear quickened her pulse. Like the man from the alley, Ty McIntyre would hurt her if she wasn't careful.

She intended to be very careful.

"I'm tired," she claimed. "You can both leave."

But she couldn't see if they complied. Black enveloped her, broken only by sparks of blue, the same dark blue as his eyes.

I have to get her out of here before he finds her!

That was his last thought, flitting through her mind, before wood snapped against wood as the door closed behind him and the doctor. Not that distance made Irina's ability to read minds any weaker. She could be miles away and the connection just as strong as if she stood face-to-face. But usually those people had some relationship to her, like her mother, her sisters or other people who'd meant something to her. Except for the killer. And this man, Ty McIntyre, who might not want to kill her but whose connection with her was stronger than any other.

She tugged at her wrist again, but the restraint refused to give. All her struggle and she'd only worked the fabric-and-Velcro strap a tiny bit looser.

She had to find a way to free herself and get the hell out of here. Because she knew if she didn't get out of the hospital soon, she would probably wind up in the morgue. If there was even anything left of her to examine…

The strangest sensation washed over Ty, lifting the hair on the nape of his neck. He glanced around the hallway, but the young doctor had left him. No one else stood in the wide corridor. Two nurses worked the station at the end, one on the phone, the other checking charts. Neither of them was the least bit aware of his presence. So no one watched him, yet that sensation persisted, prickling the skin between his shoulder blades as if someone's gaze bored into him.

He checked the doors along the hall. They were all shut tight in the jambs, leaving no space through which someone could peer out. Maybe his instincts had gotten rusty since his suspension—maybe that was why Roarke had escaped him not once but twice. Roarke wouldn't beat him again. The maniac would have to kill Ty before he'd get to Irina.

Irina...

His stomach muscles tightened as he relived his brief encounter with her. He should have been prepared for her appearance. She had the delicately featured face, the curly hair and the big Gypsy eyes, exactly as her oldest sister had described her. Yet she hadn't looked as lost as Elena's visions had led him to believe she'd look.

Despite the sedative the doctor had said she'd been administered, awareness had sparkled in Irina's dark eyes. Briefly. Then she'd gotten a strange unfocused expression on her face, as if she'd suddenly gone blind. And that was when his skin had first begun to prickle as if someone were closer to him than they'd ever been. Her sisters each had a supernatural gift—or curse, as they'd first called their abilities. Did Irina have some special ability, too?

The police officer who'd brought her here after she ran screaming into traffic had called her a wacko. Ty had found her through his old contacts and his constant monitoring of his police radio. She'd been right here in Barrett, living on the streets he'd searched over and over again for her. According to his old friend, she was either drugged out of her mind or stark-raving mad, blathering hysterically about reading a killer's mind. Even though the psychiatrist hadn't admitted it, he could tell she thought Irina was delusional, too.

But Ty knew she spoke the truth, at least about the killer; he wasn't sure about the mind-reading part. At the moment, her ability, whatever it was or wasn't, didn't matter. All that mattered was Donovan Roarke's determination to kill her.

Ty glanced at the preoccupied women at the nurses' station, then again at the empty corridor. Despite the lock on the door separating the psychiatric ward from the rest of the hospital and the locks on the individual rooms, someone clever, with the right connections, could get to Irina pretty easily. She wasn't safe here. He had to get her out.

He could do it the right way—get Elena and Ariel down here to identify and claim their sister. But they hadn't seen her in twenty years. To verify the connection between the sisters, they'd have to take a DNA test, then wait for the results. Confirmation could take at least a month. If they used the same lab the Barrett PD did, probably longer. Irina didn't have that kind of time, not with Roarke stalking her. From what she'd told the police and the psychiatrist, the madman had nearly caught her…just as Elena had envisioned. Except that Irina hadn't been too weak to fight him off. This time.

Ty couldn't give Roarke a second chance to grab her; he had to get her out. *Tonight.*

"Officer McIntyre," a soft feminine voice called out his name.

He glanced at Irina's door, but it was still closed tight, the heavy steel too insulated for her voice to carry through it. She was also strapped to the bed, trapped and helpless. Unless what else she'd told the officers was true—she could read people's minds.

The hair lifted on his neck again. Was she

reading his mind? No, he'd locked out everyone, even his best friend, for too many years for someone to slip inside his head without his realizing it.

An echo of a little girl's voice whispered from the depths of his buried memories. But time had undoubtedly distorted the facts; *he* had no special ability. He couldn't hear anyone inside his head.

"Officer McIntyre," the psychiatrist called out again as she stepped from another patient's room and closed the door behind herself. Metal jangled as she slipped keys into the pocket of her white coat. The hospital, in the old area of Barrett, was antiquated, their budget too meager for updating. Most doors were locked and unlocked the old-fashioned way. "You're still here. Did you change your mind? Is Jane Doe the woman you're looking for?"

From the flirtatious gleam in her dark eyes and the coy lift of her lips, she was asking him something else entirely—if his interest in Irina Cooper was personal, not professional. Or if he had an interest in her, the doctor.

He shook his head. "No. She's not the woman I'm looking for."

He was dedicated to finding her for her sisters, for the sake of saving her from Roarke, but not for himself. He didn't need anyone and he fully intended to keep his life that way. Single.

She smiled and tucked a strand of dark hair that had escaped her braid behind her ear. "Then…why are you still here?"

His gut twisted as he considered leading her on with lies and sweet talk. But he'd never wasted time practicing either. So he'd probably make a fool of himself trying to make a fool of her. He drew in a bracing breath. "I told you I'm a police officer, but I didn't tell you that I'm suspended from duty."

Her smile remained even as the gleam in her eyes dimmed. "I know. Since you didn't have your badge, I called the precinct before I brought you in to see her. Your lieutenant explained your suspension."

"He did?" Ty couldn't explain it himself, couldn't remember all the details of his last day on the job. He had been doing a favor for Ariel, checking on one of her students. After that…

"He told me you might have another reason for being here besides looking for someone's lost sister. All you need for reinstatement to active duty is a psychiatric evaluation." She paused and studied him before asking, "Is that why you're still here?"

The idea of someone messing with his head,

invading his thoughts and dredging up his past
had bile rising in his throat. He swallowed it down
before nodding. God, he hated putting himself out
there. And if it were only his future he had to
consider, he wouldn't.

"I guess it's time," he conceded, holding in the
sigh that expanded his lungs.

"You know, it's going to take more than one
session for a complete evaluation."

He hoped it would take only one session for
him to plan how to get Irina out. He nodded his
agreement, unable to spit out the words. But then
he asked, "So why'd you let me into her room
when you knew I was suspended?"

She smiled. "Your lieutenant vouched for you
and your integrity."

A muscle twitched in his cheek as guilt flared. But
his lieutenant knew about the witch hunt, even
though he didn't entirely believe in it. They'd had to
bring in the police after the attempt on Ariel's life and
then when Elena's daughter had been kidnapped.
Both those incidents could have been avoided if Ty
had acted faster than Roarke. He couldn't take the
chance of the guy beating him to Irina. Again.

Irina awoke to night. Or at least she assumed it
was. No sunshine penetrated the shade and heavy

drapes on the window. Not even an artificial light glowed. She could have been enveloped in the blackness of other people's thoughts, but not a single spark glittered. And the only thoughts in her head were her own, full of fear and frustration.

How long had she slept? Minutes? Hours? Days? With the drugs pumping through the IV into her veins, she had no concept of time. She would have blamed months of malnutrition instead of sedatives for her exhaustion, but she was too desperate to waste time on sleep…unless she was drugged.

She flexed her wrists, her tendons pressing against the straps that pinched her skin. She had to figure out a way to get the psychiatrist to remove the restraints. Whenever she'd spoken last to the young woman, Irina had fought to remain calm even as frustration had nagged at her. She couldn't waste any more time trying to convince the doctor of her sanity. The killer was coming for her.

Sparks flickered before her eyes, glowing like embers on a dying fire, then his voice spoke inside her head. *I have to get the charm before I get any weaker. I have to kill her. And now I know where she is. So close. So helpless…*

Goose bumps rose as her skin chilled. Her breath

shuddered out of her lungs, but the pressure on her chest didn't ease. She fought against the panic. She couldn't give in to hysteria if she hoped to ever have the restraints removed. She dragged in deep breaths through her nose, trying to calm herself.

But a big hand closing over her mouth and nose cut off her breath. Oh God, she'd slept too long. She'd missed her opportunity to escape. She had nowhere to run, nowhere to hide. Not anymore.

He'd found her again. And he had her now.

Chapter 3

"Shh…" murmured a deep voice close to her ear, warm breath stirring her hair across her cheek.

Irina thrashed her head on the pillow, trying to shake his hand from her mouth, but he held tight, his palm warm, like his breath, against her lips. She couldn't open her mouth, couldn't scream, couldn't bite. And her arms, bound to the bed, provided her no defense. She was entirely helpless.

Physically.

Mentally she might be able to read his intentions. But she dare not close her eyes, dare not invite the blackness into her mind that already enveloped her body.

"You have to trust me," he whispered, his voice a soft rasp.

She shivered, her apprehension not lessened even though she knew he wasn't the man from the alley.

"I'm going to protect *you.*"

Because he'd failed someone else? He didn't say anything either aloud or in his head to confirm her suspicion, but instinctively Irina knew that he had. And that failure haunted him, driving him to *never* fail again. So when he said he'd protect her, he meant it.

"But I have to get you out of here."

Before Donovan Roarke does.

Her heart clenched. Donovan Roarke. That was the name of the man whose evil thoughts filled her mind, whose evil deeds had traumatized her, damning her to a life of insanity…until this man, his voice whispering inside her head, had pulled her back from the edge. Ty McIntyre.

She jerked her chin up and down in an anxious nod of agreement. She had to get out of the hospital. She knew Roarke was coming for her and she couldn't get out by herself. She couldn't even get up from the bed.

"You trust me?" he asked.

She moved her head in another nod, her mouth sliding over his palm. In the silence, his breath audibly caught, and his eyes glowed bright, like a blue beacon in the darkness. She was glad that *he* couldn't read *her* mind, because once he got her out, she intended to run again. From him.

"You have to do what I say. *Everything* that I say," he insisted.

While she'd forgotten chunks of her life, even before the past few months, she remembered that she'd never done well at following orders. Maybe that was another reason her adoptive parents hadn't been able to love her.

"I'm going to take my hand away. If you scream, I won't be able to get you out of here." *I won't be able to save you.*

Because he'd be in a jail and she'd be here. Alone. At the mercy of a madman.

Come on, Irina, trust me. That last thought, and his hand lifted from her mouth, hovering just an inch away from her lips as he waited for her to scream. While he requested *her* trust, he didn't give *his*.

"I'm not crazy," she assured him in a soft whisper.

He moved his hand from her face to her wrist and the restraint binding her to the bed. "I know." *I know everything.*

And there was so much she didn't know—
about herself, about her sisters, about the witch
hunt. But what she wanted most to learn couldn't
wait until he'd set her free. "Who are you?"

"Ty McIntyre."

She hadn't forgotten the psychiatrist's intro-
duction. But his name told her nothing. "*Who* are
you to *me?*"

Why had his thoughts pushed into her mind
before she'd ever met him? What was their connection?

"I'm a friend."

Pieces of her past were missing, so much she'd
forgotten or lost to drugs and alcohol. But if he'd
been a friend, she would have remembered him. Ty
McIntyre wasn't the type of man any woman could
forget. Instead of screaming *Liar!* at him, as she had
at the killer, she just whispered, "No, you're not."

"I'm here for your sisters." *For you.*

"You're working for them?" Donovan Roarke
had claimed the same thing.

"They're friends of mine," he said. "I'm going
to bring you to them, but we have to hurry."

"Yes." She expelled a nervous breath. Her
sisters were part of that missing past. Only faint
memories of them remained, like faded photo-
graphs in an old album.

"We have to hurry," she agreed. "*He* knows where I am."

He didn't doubt her certainty, either aloud or in his head. He just uttered the man's name with the intensity of a curse. "Roarke."

"If he's the one…"

Who killed your mother. Your aunts. Who tried to kill your sisters and niece. "He's the one."

Scream after scream echoed through her mind. All the pain. All the horror. She trembled under the force.

"Don't be afraid," he told her.

For so long she'd known nothing but fear…except for when she'd lost all touch with reality. And she'd done that too long, giving up when she should have been fighting.

The thought flickered through her mind that maybe she should be fighting *him*…despite his intentions. He might want to protect her, but she had no way of knowing if he would be able to keep his promise. She didn't know him. Yet somehow he seemed so familiar to her….

The restraints undone, he helped her from the bed. As she reached for the IV, pulling it from her arm, his fingers fumbled with the ties holding her gown together in the back.

Her breath hissed out as his knuckles brushed her bare skin. "Hey—"

"Shh…it's okay," he assured her. "You can't go out there in this."

"But…"

"I brought other clothes." Before the cool air did more than brush her naked skin, he pulled a scratchy cotton shirt over her head, dressing her as if she were a child. Or helpless. She wouldn't be helpless anymore.

"Let me," she protested, fumbling in the darkness for the pants. But as she lifted her leg to pull them on, dizziness overwhelmed her, and she swayed…only a few inches before her back settled against his solid chest. His arms came around her, helping her tug up the pants of the scrubs he must have stolen for her, his fingers fast and sure as he stretched the elastic waistband over her hips.

Heat streaked through Irina's stomach at the brush of his knuckles against her navel, the brush of his hard body against her softness. Her limbs still weak, she melted deeper into his warmth, into his strength.

"Irina…" His breath stirred her hair again, then his fingers as he tunneled them into her thick curls.

"What…?"

"A braid," he said as if concentrating on his task. And perhaps he was, because she could pull no other thought from his mind despite their closeness.

"Ty?" She used just his name to question his action, not wanting anyone to overhear their conversation and learn she was awake and not alone.

Intent on her hair, he murmured, "The psychiatrist."

"She's helping?"

"Yes, but she doesn't know it," he admitted. "You're going to *be* her."

It wouldn't be the first time she'd been someone she wasn't. But she wanted it to be the last. She wanted to be Irina Cooper now. For as long as she lived.

He knelt in the darkness, and Irina felt his big hands on her feet, his skin warm against hers as he peeled off the slipper socks to pull on canvas shoes. She reached out, dizzy again, and used his broad shoulders to steady herself. Muscles rippled beneath her hands. Then he stood, his body bumping against hers.

Dizziness lightened her head again as awareness rushed through her, quickening her pulse. She dragged in a deep breath, his scent of mint and soap so fresh and clean, unlike where she'd been, what she'd been.

"And here's her jacket," he said, sliding the sleeves over the scrubs she wore.

A plastic tag dug into Irina's breast while something heavy dragged down the coat pocket and knocked hard against her thigh.

"You have the keys."

She'd like to know how he'd gotten them, but she couldn't waste time asking, nor did it really matter. Getting out before Roarke got in was all that mattered.

"You have to let me in and out of this room and the ward and act like you're her," he instructed.

"But…"

"The hospital's old. Dimly lit. The nurses' station a distance away. We can do this, Irina." He expelled a ragged breath. "I keep calling you Irina. You remember you have sisters, so you must remember—"

"My name?" Despite the fierce knocking of her heart against her ribs, she smiled. "I wouldn't have asked who you are if I didn't know who I am."

"So you *are* faking."

"Amnesia? Some of it's real." But she was still having trouble with that, with distinguishing what was and what wasn't real.

Was he? She reached out, sliding her hand along the soft bristle of day-old beard on his hard jaw. Her pulse raced at the jolt of awareness, of recognition, that overwhelmed her. She heard his thoughts again.

God, he was asking too much of her, expecting too much. She wasn't like Ariel and Elena.

Her sisters. He thought of her sisters, and in comparison, she didn't measure up. She pulled her hand back from his face and curled her fingers into a fist to stop the tingling. Of course she wouldn't measure up. She knew where she was, what she had become.

He asked, "Can you do this?"

"Act like the psychiatrist?" She would have been one…if she hadn't lost track of reality. "Yeah, I can do that."

She'd do anything to get out of the hospital before the killer got in…even trust a man who scared her as much as Ty McIntyre did.

Ty held his breath as Irina fumbled with the keys, locking her empty room behind them. At the end of the hall, one of the nurses glanced up from the desk at the station. Irina lifted her hand in a brief wave. The nurse paused, then waved back. "You're here late, Dr. Kimber," she called out.

Nerves twisted Ty's guts into knots. God, it was over. This quickly. From a distance, Irina

could pass for the dark-haired, dark-eyed doctor.
But her voice…

She coughed as if clearing her throat. Ty dared
not touch her or even whisper the warning burning
his mind. *Don't answer back. Don't.*

She must *not* have been able to read minds, as
she'd told the police and the psychiatrist, because
she spoke. "Officer McIntyre wanted to double-
check that Jane Doe isn't the girl he's looking for."

"She isn't," Ty said, taking Irina's hand as if to
shake it. "Thank you for coming back tonight,
Doctor." He tugged her down the hall, away from
the nurses' station. "I don't want to keep you."

And hopefully neither would her coworker.

"How is she?" the nurse called out. "Does she
need anything?"

Irina shook her head, then murmured the name
of a drug and the number of milligrams she'd administered through Jane's IV. "She should sleep
through the night."

"What do you think is wrong with her?" the
nurse asked, rising from her chair at the desk. Her
shoes squeaked against the worn linoleum.

Ty's breath caught. He couldn't believe that
Irina had pulled off the disguise as well as she had.
But if the woman got any closer, their duplicity
would be discovered for sure. He'd broken into the

doctor's locker and stolen her keys and coat for nothing.

As the woman walked closer, Irina stepped deeper in the shadows of the poorly lit hall, then gestured toward him. "Let me walk Officer McIntyre out first," she said, jingling the keys in her hand.

"Of course," the nurse said, turning back toward the station.

Ty expelled a ragged breath as they headed toward the other end of the corridor, where locked doors separated the psychiatric ward from the rest of the old hospital.

"We're not out yet," Irina said, clenching the keys in her hand. "I don't know which one...."

Neither had she for her room, but she'd found it fast enough to not draw too much attention to them. "Try the big ones first," he advised.

She bent her head and focused on her task, her bottom lip pulled between her teeth. The tip of the first key struck the opening of the chamber but wouldn't slide inside. The second slid in but wouldn't turn the lock. When she reached for the third, the nurse called out again.

Ty glanced over his shoulder, and his heart slammed into his ribs. She'd gotten up from the desk and walked toward them. "Having trouble, Dr. Kimber?"

Irina shook her head, tossing the braid he'd haphazardly pulled together in the dark back and forth across her back as if whipping herself. "No, it's just hard to see in the hall," she called back, then cleared her throat again and added, "They have to get more light in here someday."

"Electrical system's too old, like everything else around here," the nurse commented, patting her head of graying hair. A rueful smile lifted her lips. "Except for you young interns and residents."

The lock clicked as Irina turned the third key. She reached for the knob, her hand shaking. "I'll be right back," she told the nurse as she slipped ahead of Ty into the outside hall. A bank of elevators stood across from them, the dull metallic doors shut tight. Ty strode over and slapped the down arrow while she relocked the door to the psychiatric ward. The keys rattled as her hands shook.

"You're doing great," he murmured when she joined him in staring at the doors. He glanced toward her, then to the stairwell beyond her. Dare he wait for the elevator?

"How far up are we?" she asked, her voice unsteady with nerves.

"Top floor. Eighteenth."

Her mouth, her lips naturally red and full, pulled into a grimace. "A lot of stairs."

"A lot of stairs," he agreed as he pulled his gaze from her and concentrated on the elevator light. He couldn't afford the distraction of a woman who could look the way she did with no makeup. Her lashes were naturally thick and long, framing those big, dark eyes, while her honey-toned skin revealed not a single flaw.

Was she really the same woman Elena had envisioned in the alley, unkempt and out of her mind?

Behind them, the knob rattled on the door to the psych ward. "She realized I'm not Dr. Kimber," Irina said, her dark eyes widening in alarm.

Ty grabbed her hand and pulled her toward the stairwell. "Come on. We gotta get out of here."

Automatic hinges held open the door to the stairs just long enough that Ty caught the arrival of the elevator and the man stepping out. He had dark red hair and eyes that burned with hatred and madness. "Oh God!"

He shoved Irina toward the stairs, gasping an anxious, "Run!"

Even though her feet hit the steps, she peered up and around him. Ty didn't know if she caught a glimpse of Roarke before the door closed. He was more concerned about Roarke catching a glimpse of them.

"Hurry!" He caught her around the waist, half carrying her as their feet skimmed over the steps, hardly touching them as they ran down flight after flight, their frantic footfalls echoing eerily in the cement stairwell. His bad leg, broken in the collapse of another staircase, throbbed with pain as his foot hitting each step jarred the still-healing bone and muscles. He gritted his teeth, biting back the pain, forcing it from his mind to focus instead on getting her to safety.

They'd fled several stories when a door slammed open above them, metal crashing against concrete. Ty didn't have to look up to know that the door was from the eighteenth floor and the person joining their mad dash was Donovan Roarke.

"You can't save her!" the deranged killer yelled, his voice a harsh shout in the confined area. "All you'll do is die with her, McIntyre."

From his years on the force, Ty knew there was no sense in trying to deal with a lunatic. He didn't care about Roarke's threats against him; his total focus was on Irina. Her arm slid around his waist, her fingers clenched in his shirt as he dragged her along with him. In their haste to escape the hospital and the killer, they fell against the metal railing and bounced off the cement-block walls. Each crash jolted his leg, the pain traveling through his limb like an electrical shock. But he couldn't slow down.

"You're not a witch, McIntyre. You don't deserve to die like they do. Give her to me and I'll let you live," Roarke yelled out his bargain between ragged pants for breath.

Ty's life for hers? Irina had family who cared about her, who loved her. It wasn't a fair trade.

"Go to hell," Ty shouted back. Roarke didn't need his condemnation, though. His actions were certain to send him there, but Ty fully intended to expedite his trip.

"I gave you a chance," Roarke said as if resigned, then he fired.

Bullets sprayed against the concrete walls, raining dusty bits of cement onto them as they ran. "Come on," Ty said, rushing Irina down the last flight. His hand closed over hers on the knob of the door to the first floor; together they turned it.

From the corner of his eye Ty glimpsed Roarke, flights above them, leaning over the railing, taking aim, his Glock directed at them. His hand over her head, Ty pushed Irina down as he ducked. Bullets bounced off the metal frame over them as they crawled through the partially open doorway. On the other side, Ty shoved his shoulder against the steel door, fighting the automatic hinge to push it closed. More shots fired, only the door separating the bullets from his body as the metal protruded from each hit.

"Come on!" he commanded Irina, his hand wrapped around hers as he propelled them both through the lobby, deserted at this late hour. Antique furnishings sat empty but for a faint film of dust. An old turnstile door stood between them and the canopy-covered entrance. Ty jammed them both into one section, her body soft and warm as she trembled against him.

"It's okay," he assured her even as more shots rang out behind them. The thick plastic of the turnstile splintered from the bullets. Ty bent over Irina, sheltering her with his body as they shoved the door forward, then stumbled out onto the sidewalk. He kept her close, her feet hardly touching the asphalt as he ran across the dimly lit lot to where he'd left his truck parked.

Hand shaking, he fumbled with his keys, clicking the automatic locks. When she moved to head around the passenger's side, he held tight to her jacket, lifting and pushing her through the driver's door and onto the seat. "Stay low."

More shots rang out behind them, breaking the

quiet of the night. Then, in the distance, sirens whined. At least someone had called the police. On him for helping a patient escape the psychiatric ward? Or on the madman who relentlessly pursued them, firing shot after shot at them?

Ty jammed the key into the ignition, his hand reaching for the shifter before the truck engine even sprang to life. He slammed into Reverse, tires bouncing over the curb as he pulled out of the parking spot and into the drive.

"Keep low," he ordered Irina again as she lifted her head. He doubted she was trying to glance out the windows, though. She had that look in her eyes, that glazed-over, unfocused gaze of someone blind.

But his skin didn't prickle; it wasn't his mind she was trying to read—if telepathy was her ability. God, he could keep her safe from Roarke's actions—or at least try—but he couldn't keep her safe from the madman's thoughts. He pushed her down, her face in his lap, her breath warm through the denim covering his thighs.

The rear window shattered, shards of glass biting into the back of his head and his neck, then raining down over them and the leather seat. "Son of a—"

He jerked the wheel, sending the truck careening back and forth across the driving lanes as he steered for the street. A moving target was harder to hit.

"Are you okay?" she asked, her voice thready with fear and adrenaline. "Did he shoot you?"

"No." But blood trickled down the back of his neck from the glass splinters embedded in his skin, the sting of the cuts a faint echo of the pain throbbing in his leg.

She moved her head against his leg, but he pressed his hand on her shoulder, holding her down, out of range of the bullets and broken glass. "Ty," she said, the fatality of her tone drawing his attention before she added, "He's going to kill you."

Ty glanced in the rearview mirror, at the lights dropping farther and farther behind them. He patted her shoulder. "We're losing him. We're going to be fine."

She drew in a shaky breath. "You have to believe me, no matter how crazy this sounds. But I can *hear* his thoughts."

Ty's guts knotted. Oh God, she *had* been inside Roarke's head. "Irina—"

"Please believe me," she urged him. "I'm not crazy. I'm not crazy."

She didn't seem as certain of that as he was, though. "Irina, I believe you."

Her face, flushed before from their mad dash down eighteen flights, paled now with shock. Had no one ever believed in her before? Or was it Roarke's thoughts that filled her with fear? He stroked his hand up her shoulder to her neck, kneading the tense muscles. "What did you hear, Irina?"

Her breath shuddered out. "He's going to kill you!"

Despite her concern, Ty couldn't fight the grin lifting half his mouth as he agreed, "He's trying."

So had a lot of other men, but no one had succeeded. Yet. He glanced down at the woman lying across his lap. Her big, dark eyes, focused again and full of fear, stared up at him. Something shifted in his chest; his heart clenched as if he felt *her* fear. It wasn't his—he hadn't been afraid in a long time. Not for himself.

Unless…was he afraid *of* her? And if he wasn't, maybe he should be, because if she could read Roarke's mind, she could probably read his, too.

And there were things in his head that no one else should know. There were things in his head he wished *he* didn't know.

The witch was going to get him killed. Didn't he realize that? Ty McIntyre wasn't like his friend and the other man, who were in love with witches. He didn't even know this woman. Why would he come to her aid? Why would he interfere in Roarke's plan? In the vendetta?

Roarke fisted his hands on the steering wheel and pressed harder on the accelerator. But his old van couldn't gain ground on McIntyre's pickup. He glanced at the dash, where the speedometer needle trembled but wouldn't push forward any more.

His white orderly uniform reflected back from the dash, glowing in the dim light. His plan had been solid, well thought out. If not for McIntyre's interference, it would have been well executed.

Now the police officer would be executed. By Roarke. Regret rose like bile in his throat, but he swallowed it down. He'd killed more than the witches. He'd killed others who'd gotten in his way.

But he'd never killed a police officer, a comrade. A man who, like him, had sworn to serve and protect. Was that the reason for his interference? That even suspended, McIntyre couldn't take off the badge, he couldn't stop serving and protecting?

Or was it more? Was there some connection between the witch and the cop?

He shook his head. It didn't matter what was between McIntyre and the witch; it wouldn't last.

Donovan hated to do it, but McIntyre had ignored his generous offer. And for his rejection, he would have to pay…with his life.

Roarke had planned to kill the witch next. But McIntyre had left him no choice.

The suspended police officer with the white-knight complex would be the next to *die*.

Chapter 4

Hatred filled Irina, twisting her heart and sickening her stomach. Thoughts rolled through her head like heat waves off hot asphalt. So much anger, such deadly intent. Even with her eyes open, blackness blinded her. Sparks of red glinted in the darkness stretched before her like droplets of spattered blood.

Ty's blood.

"He's going to kill you," she said again, her words a whisper, her throat dry with fear.

His thigh tensed beneath her cheek as he pressed down the accelerator, and the truck shot forward, bouncing along the rutted street leading away from the old hospital. His hand touched her head, his fingers tangling in the tendrils escaping her braid.

"Don't worry about me," he assured her. "I am—I was—a police officer."

"So was he." She'd just learned that from the madman's latest thoughts.

"Donovan Roarke was a disgrace to the badge." *But then, maybe so was I.*

More anger rolled through Irina, this time Ty's. Silence fell between them, broken only by the wind whipping through the shattered window and by the roar of the motor as he raced along the streets of Barrett, continuing to stretch the distance between them and the killer.

The darkness faded. Ty's thoughts didn't blind her anymore, not like the killer's. Probably the way they'd worked together for her escape had strengthened their connection.

Drawing in a deep breath, Irina braced her hand on his knee, almost bare through the worn denim of his jeans, and she pushed herself up from her prone position. "Where are we?" she asked.

He knew; he didn't have to think about it, so she had no idea. They passed houses, mostly dark at this hour except for ones where porch lights burned, casting shadows onto the vehicles parked at the curb. Then the houses gave way to businesses as they headed deeper into the heart of the city of Barrett.

"Where are you taking me?"

Elena and Ariel will be so relieved. So happy.

"No!" she said before he even told her. "You can't take me to them!"

"To who? Where do you think I'm taking you?" he asked. *Does she know? Or is she as delusional as the psychiatrist had thought? But the doctor had also made some incorrect assumptions about me, during our session.*

What assumptions? Their session? Reading his mind gave Irina no answers, only more questions.

"Ty, I *know* what you're thinking." She scooted along the bench seat, away from his heat and intensity. The cold wind whipped around her and through the thin cotton of the white coat and scrubs, chilling her to the bone. "I'm not delusional. I'm…"

What had her mother called it twenty years ago, that fateful night Irina and her sisters had been taken from her? Irina had been so young, too young to remember the details that had haunted her memory for so many years. She turned toward him, studying his profile illuminated by the dashboard lights. "Cursed?"

His lips twitched into that half grin she'd glimpsed before, when she'd first told him of Roarke's intention to kill him. What kind of man felt amusement rather than fear over a threat to his life? One as crazy as she'd been?

His raspy voice soft with affection, he shared, "Ariel used to call herself that, too."

"Cursed." The description was milder than what she'd thought before, for so long—that she was *damned*. To a life of insanity. "I can read people's minds."

"You're telepathic," he said as if the ability over which she'd tortured herself for years was perfectly normal. "And your oldest sister, Elena, sees the future. And Ariel—" again affection softened his voice "—sees ghosts. You're all—"

"Cursed." He'd been about to say *gifted*, but she couldn't think of herself that way, not yet, not when her life had been such a nightmare, courtesy of Donovan Roarke…and the vendetta he'd resurrected. Fear pressed on her chest, shortening her breath while quickening her heartbeat. "There's so much I don't know…or maybe I did and I can't remember…."

"That's why I'm bringing you to your sisters. They can explain everything to you."

While he walked away from her and focused on

Roarke. She didn't have to read his mind to know his intention—leaving her to the care of her sisters while he concentrated on finding the killer. But what if Roarke found him first? Would Ty survive with his life?

She reached across the seat and clasped his forearm. Muscles hardened beneath her fingers. "No, you can't bring me there. I *can't* meet them."

"Irina—"

"Not like this."

"You look—"

"It's not how I *look*. It's how I *feel*. I can't see them yet." She bit her lip, drawing in a deep breath as she struggled with the pride that had abandoned her for so long but now threatened to rule her. She'd have to tell them where she'd been, how she'd been living…or not living. "I'm still a mess, Ty."

"You're not," he insisted. "You were great back at the hospital—"

"He would have killed me," she said, fear shaking her voice. To quell their trembling, she tightened her fingers around Ty's arm. He was so strong, so solid. "If not for you, *he* would have taken me out of there. He would have killed anyone in his way." That doctor she'd impersonated, probably the nurse. "Where do you think he is now?"

Ty's gaze lifted to the rearview mirror, as it had so often since he'd pealed out of the parking lot. "He's not behind us. I lost him a long time ago."

"So where do you think he is?" She knew, but she needed to force Ty to admit the killer's whereabouts. "You're a police officer. You must know."

His chin, dark with stubble, jerked in a rough nod. "Outside Elena's or Ariel's."

She shivered as the wind whipped around her shoulders and fear fluttered in her heart. "Waiting for us."

"Probably."

"You risked your life for me once tonight." Her fingers flexed against Ty's arm, but she didn't release him. She'd hold on to him physically if she had to. "I don't want you to risk it again."

"Irina—"

"I don't want to put *them* in danger, either." Her sisters. Could she say it? Could she believe she had family, real family? She'd been alone for so long.

"Ariel and Elena want to see you so badly. They've been so worried about you—"

"I know." As he had, their voices had called her back. They wanted her—but not her alone. They wanted the charm, too. "But I don't have it."

He glanced over at her as if alarmed by her last comment. *Is she okay?*

She couldn't blame him for his continued doubts about her sanity. She had them, too. Even as she resurfaced from the hell in which she'd been immersed much of the past few months, she struggled with the doubts.

"I don't have the charm," she explained, her voice choked with regret. She released his arm and leaned back against the seat, her shoulders sagging. "The charm they think they need. The one he wants. I don't have it. I don't even know if I remember it…."

"A moon. It was a little crescent moon made out of pewter or something that looks like it."

Tears stung her eyes as she remembered her mother pressing the sliver of moon into her palm, then her oldest sister clasping it to her bracelet. She and her sisters had been taken away from their mother that night twenty years ago, and she'd been separated from them and put into foster care. While the authorities had taken them away, their mother must have given up her parental rights or else the Bowerses wouldn't have been able to adopt her. Had Mama given up Elena and Ariel or just her? Had her own mother been unable to love Irina as the Bowerses had been unable to love her?

She blinked the tears from her eyes and cleared them from her throat, determined to stop feeling sorry for herself. Then she told him, "I don't have the charm."

She refused to meet her sisters until she found it—*if* she could find it. Had she lost it long ago? Her stomach clenched. What if she'd sold or traded it for booze or drugs?

"You were only four or five when you were taken away from your family." He came to her defense, as he had at the hospital. "It's no wonder you lost it."

Not just the charm but her sanity. Was that what he thought? She couldn't get inside his mind...not when she was so deep inside her own, burying herself under recriminations and regrets.

He reached across the seat and closed his hand around hers. Despite the cold night air blowing around them through the broken window, his skin was warm against hers. "It's okay. They want you. Just *you*."

"No, they don't," she insisted. "They want the charm. They need the charm."

And by losing it, she'd let them down. She remembered their thoughts; they'd been counting on her to still have it in her possession.

Ty's raspy voice firm with confidence, he assured her, "We'll find the charm."

"You'll help me find it?" No one had ever

helped her...until tonight, until he'd broken her out of the psychiatric ward minutes before Donovan Roarke had arrived. When she'd been living on the street, she'd been invisible, no one seeing her, noticing her distress and her desperation.

Ty nodded and squeezed her hand. "Yes."

Roarke's threats echoed in her mind. "He's going to kill you."

"Don't worry about me," he dismissed her concern. "I'm not easy to kill."

Another old memory teased her. Lights flashing, the rattle of wheels as a stretcher rushed down a hallway, propelled by anxious paramedics. Blood. And pain. So much pain. She closed her eyes, reeling. The memory might have been old, but the pain was fresh and overwhelming.

"You're exhausted," he said. "And probably still drugged. How'd you know what was in that IV, anyway?"

"I was studying to become a psychiatrist." She clearly remembered that part of her life. "I graduated early from high school and college."

His lips tipped up into that crooked grin again. "Because you *knew* the answers."

She'd been motivated, too, to become a psychiatrist so she could figure out what was wrong with

her. "I was almost finished with med school…"
When she'd heard her mother's scream, when the
witch hunt had begun again.

"What happened?" he asked. "How'd you wind
up…where you did?"

"On the streets?" She sighed. "I lived there
before, when I ran away."

"When you were a kid?"

She nodded. God, she'd been a hellion in her
teens. Rebellious. Angry. And so damned confused.
Even after she'd grown up and for a while had
gotten her life on track, the confusion had remained.

"You ran away from your adoptive parents?" he
asked as if genuinely interested in her. Hadn't he
only been doing a favor for friends? He didn't
really care about her.

But still she found herself answering him,
telling him things she hadn't shared with anyone.
"My parents—my adoptive parents—didn't want
me to know that I wasn't theirs."

"But you knew?" *She knew everything. How
could someone live like that, inundated with the
thoughts and fears of everyone else?*

"Sometimes I can't live like this," she answered
his unspoken question. "That's why I break
down." Or use drugs and alcohol to truly black out.
"It's too hard, too much…."

"I'm sorry, Irina. You're exhausted." His hand, so big and warm enveloping hers, gave another reassuring squeeze. "I won't keep pushing. I'll take you home—"

"No!" she shouted, pulling her hand from his. "He knows who you are, where you live—"

"Damn." *She was right. If Roarke wasn't waiting at David's penthouse or Joseph's estate, he'd be parked outside Ty's place. Waiting. Ty hadn't come this close to getting Irina to safety in order to give up now.*

She realized Roarke had been close—twice—to taking her. To carrying out his gruesome intentions, his witch hunt. She shuddered.

"Give me a minute to think," Ty murmured. The houses. He had more than one. He didn't rent the apartment in the three-family where he lived. He owned the entire house. But no one knew that, not even his best friend. No one knew what he'd inherited from his father's estate. The properties. Most of them occupied. But one. Could he take her there? Could he go back there himself?

Irina's stomach knotted with the revulsion gripping Ty. She studied his profile, his jaw clenched hard, his deep blue eyes gleaming. He turned toward her, probably feeling her scrutiny. One of his dark brows, a tiny scar splitting it, lifted above his left eye.

His throat moved as he swallowed hard, then asked, "Can you really read my mind?"

She nodded.

His breath audibly caught. "And I can't shut you out?"

As he had everyone else? Even his best friend? She shook her head. "No."

He sighed, a ragged expulsion of air. "Damn." He had more to fear from her than Donovan Roarke.

"I won't hurt you," she assured him. At least not intentionally.

But why would he worry about her when he wasn't concerned about a man intent on killing him? Obviously his secrets were more important to him than his life.

He drove for a while longer, his mind carefully blank. The air in the truck vibrated from the tense silence. She sighed and conceded, "I guess you *can* shut me out."

Used to the sharp turns he'd made to avoid being tailed, she didn't notice that he'd pulled into someplace until a garage door opened. Then the old wood door rattled as it closed behind them, shutting them into a dark space illuminated only by the headlamps glinting off the bare planks of the back wall. Without the wind whistling through the cab, the silence was total and eerie. Even without the wind, the cold cut deep like a sharp knife.

She should have paid more attention to where he'd taken her. Back at the hospital, she'd intended to run from him once he'd helped her escape the psychiatric ward. But after he'd shielded her with his body, she'd stopped fearing him.

Now she was afraid *for* him. Not only because of Roarke's deadly intentions but because for the first time fear emanated from him. When Roarke had fired shot after shot at them, she'd been the one terrified while Ty had remained fearless.

But here, in the dark, anxiety gripped his heart and hers. The man who'd had no qualms about taking a bullet for her hesitated over opening his door and stepping out into the garage of a house he owned.

"Ty, what's going on?" How had he shut her out when no one else had ever been able? She'd only been deaf to the thoughts of others when she'd drunk herself into oblivion and blacked out. Or when she'd worked hard to block them out, to be normal, as the Bowerses had wanted so badly for their daughter to be.

"You stay here," he said, his voice a hoarse rasp. "I'll check the house and come back for you."

When he opened the truck door, she caught his arm, reluctant to let him go.

"You'll be okay," he assured her.

"It's not me I'm worried about," she admitted.

But he didn't hear her, intent on the inner demons he wrestled. "You'll be safe in here. I'll lock the door, then come back and get you after I've made sure the house is clear."

"Damn it, Ty, you should have brought her straight here," his best friend berated him. His deep voice vibrated with anger through the cell phone Ty pressed to his ear.

He should have brought her anywhere but *here*.

To make sure the house was secure, he walked from room to room. The hardwood floors creaked beneath his weight, protesting his intrusion. He'd never been welcome in this house, not when he was a kid, not even now, when he was a man. A man whose hand trembled as he flipped on light switches, a man who cringed as shadows moved.

"Ty!" The shout crackled, drawing his attention back to the phone.

"Yeah?"

"Where are you?"

Hell. He glanced around at the walls, the paint old and faded, the fist holes in the plaster crudely patched. Stale air hung heavy, dust particles dancing on it, with the echoes of old cries…of pain.

He swallowed down the bile rising in his throat, then answered his friend, "I brought her some-place Roarke will never look."

"Don't underestimate Roarke," David cautioned.

"I've made that mistake before," he conceded.

"We all have. God, it'll kill Ariel if something happened to Irina now that you've found her." And David loved his fiancée so much that her pain became his.

Ty couldn't understand loving someone like that; a connection that close was a fantasy. Not a reality. Not an old memory like those currently battering him…the way his father's fists once had. He flinched, a muscle ticking in his cheek. "*Nothing* will happen to her."

"Ty, you broke her out of the hospital. *You* broke the law." David's agitated sigh rattled the phone. "Do you know what this is going to cost you?"

"My job?" He snorted as if it didn't mean *anything* to him when for so long his career in law enforcement had been *everything* to him.

He'd become a cop out of gratitude and respect for David's father, the police officer who'd taken him into their home, their family—something he'd never really known—after Ty's dad died.

"I already lost my badge." His gun, too, which he could use now, as he jumped at shadows. Because of the ongoing investigation into the arrest that had led to a suspect's death, he'd been prohibited from carrying any weapon.

David never cut him any slack, more know-it-all older brother than sympathetic friend. "All you have to do to get reinstated is submit to a psychiatric evaluation."

Ty had done that just that afternoon. Dr. Kimber had told him to confront his past so he could deal with all those old memories. To deal with all that pain. It washed over him in waves, pulling him under like a rip current. His chest rose and fell in violent jerks as he fought for breath.

He wasn't just confronting his past, he was drowning in it.

"It might cost you more than your job, Ty."

His life, if Roarke had his way—if Irina could really hear the madman's thoughts. God, he wished she couldn't. For her sake.

"Your freedom, Ty."

He stepped into the last room off the hall. His hand shaking, he flipped the switch. A bare light-bulb dangled from a cord in the ceiling, casting shadows around the dingy little room. The closet door, standing ajar, creaked as something small scurried beneath it. Ty jumped, his heart hammering against his ribs. God, he hated this place. Those memories he'd thought buried so deep threatened to surface.

The psychiatrist hadn't been able to pull them out of him. Irina hadn't been able to read them. But all it took was stepping back inside this house…this hell.

"Ty!"

He flinched. "Yeah?"

"What the hell's going on?"

"Nothing, David. It's late. I'm making sure this place is secure." That Roarke wasn't ahead of him as he'd been for much of his witch hunt, until tonight.

"Where are you?" David asked again.

"It's better you don't know." Because David had been in this house, too. If not for David coming here that last time, Ty wouldn't be alive now. Even then, he probably still wouldn't have made it if it hadn't been for…

Her.

The little girl standing beside his stretcher, pulling him back from the brink of death. She'd had long, dark curls and big, dark eyes…and even though he hadn't said a word, hadn't even been conscious, she'd heard him. She'd felt his pain and despair. She'd spoken to him. And he'd heard her. He'd opened his eyes, blinking against the harsh lights and the pain hammering in his skull and radiating throughout his broken body. His spirit—broken, too—had mended with her encouragement, and he'd fought for the life he hadn't considered worth living anymore.

The floor creaked in the hall, and he turned to the doorway, where *she* stood, watching him. Her eyes big and dark, shimmering with unshed tears.

Her.

She could read his mind. She knew everything he'd thought, everything he'd felt since he'd stepped inside, no matter how hard he'd fought to block her from his mind. His pain made her face grow pale, darkened her eyes and quivered in her bottom lip.

David's deep voice vibrated in his ear, but he couldn't hear him. He couldn't hear anything. He flipped the phone shut and shoved it in his pocket. Then he reached for her, pulling her into his arms.

Her body trembled against his, shaking with the pain that he'd felt. "I'm sorry," he said. He shouldn't have brought her here, shouldn't have subjected her to his demons. Not only could she read minds but she was empathetic, feeling the emotions of those around her...like the little girl in the hospital.

"It was me," she whispered, her breath warm against his throat as she wound her arms around his back. "It was me. I was there. My adoptive father'd had a heart attack. My...adoptive mother left me alone in the waiting room. I saw them wheel you in. I felt your pain."

Then and now.

"God, Irina..."

What the hell was this—this connection between them that went back nearly twenty years? Coincidence? Fate?

Her trembling fingers slid along his jaw, as she'd touched him at the hospital, but now she tilted his face down to hers.

"Fate," she answered him before rising up on tiptoe and pressing her lips to his.

Ty's breath shuddered out as desire coursed through him. He slid one hand up her back to cup her head in his palm. Her hair, free of his sloppy braid, curled around his fingers like ties binding them together. The way the past bound them.

His mouth moved over hers, deepening the kiss, parting her lips. She was the sweetest thing he'd ever tasted. Her generosity and empathy enveloped him, lightening the load of pain he'd carried for so long. So alone.

"You're not alone," she murmured. "You're not alone anymore."

He pulled back, his body taut and begging for more. But he couldn't take any more from her. She was too fragile, and he'd already burdened her too much. "Irina, we can't…."

Her breath came fast through her parted lips. "Ty, I'm not…"

She didn't finish her denial, probably because she couldn't swear she wasn't as fragile as he thought.

"I can't take advantage of you," he insisted. "You're scared."

"Messed up," she corrected him, her lips lifting in a slight self-deprecating smile. "I'm messed up."

"You're not the only one," he pointed out, gesturing around at the room of his nightmares.

He hadn't stepped foot in this room since his father died. He glanced down to the boards stained with the old man's blood. God, he hadn't thought the man human…until then. Until his blood had poured out of the wound in his chest. If David hadn't rushed into the room waving his father's police service weapon, if Ty's dad hadn't reached for it, if the gun hadn't gone off…

"You'd be dead," she said, confirming what he'd already known.

His own father would have beaten him to death that day. He nearly had.

"He was a monster," she said.

Like Roarke.

Like Ty.

He'd lost control his last day on the job. He'd gone to check on a student Ariel had been worried about, a student whose ghost she'd seen—but Ty hadn't known about her gift then. He'd found the child, dead at her father's hands. And something inside of him had snapped. So much of that day was gone from his mind. He had a scar and a suspension but not much recollection of what had really happened. The girl's father had wound up as dead as his own dad.

Irina pulled out of his arms, wrapping hers around herself. She'd read his thoughts; she knew his fear. And now she feared him, too. He couldn't blame her.

"Don't," she murmured. "Don't presume to know what *I* think or what *I* feel, Ty McIntyre."

He nodded. "You're right. I don't have a gift, not like you." But he was cursed all the same.

She shook her head. "That's not what I meant. You can't presume to know what *I* don't. *I* don't know what I think. Or what I feel."

Regret bubbled up inside him, so many regrets. "You're exhausted."

She nodded. "I hope that's all it is. I hope I'm just tired. Not crazy."

"You're not crazy, Irina."

"Then why do I want to make love to a man I don't know?" she asked, her dark eyes bright with passion.

His heart slammed against his ribs at her admission, and his body hardened and throbbed, begging to take her up on her desire.

But she continued, "Why do I want to make love to a man who doesn't really know himself?"

He couldn't deny that she spoke the truth. He didn't know himself. He didn't know what he was capable of. Murder? Was he all that different from Donovan Roarke?

"Ty." She turned toward him, wrapping her hand around his to tug him from his old bedroom. "Come with me…."

She walked down the short hall toward the one furnished room. Sparsely furnished, all it had was a brass bed and a bare mattress a previous tenant had left.

"Irina, we can't do this…." She was too fragile, too confused. And, at the moment, so was he.

She walked past the bed and pushed open the

bathroom door, pulling him inside with her. "You got cut in the truck when the back window broke. I want to make sure you're okay."

He brushed a hand through his hair, knocking the bits of glass from it. "I'm okay," he said. Physically. Emotionally he hadn't been okay since he'd set foot in this house again. God, he should have gotten rid of it long ago. But it had reminded him of how far he'd come…until he'd returned.

Slim hands on his shoulders, she pushed him down so he sat on the edge of the rusted tub. Then she ran her fingers through his hair and over his scalp. He didn't notice the pain, only the heat of her touch. Like her kiss, it branded him. Like her admission of wanting to make love to him, her touch had his heart racing.

Sucking her bottom lip between her teeth, she murmured, "You have a few deep cuts. You could probably use some stitches…."

He'd had more than enough of those over the years. "We can't risk a trip to the hospital now." Because Roarke might be watching those, too, thinking he'd hit one of them with all the shots he'd fired. "But the cuts are fine, anyway. They stopped bleeding."

"Let me clean them at least," she said, opening

the door of the medicine cabinet. Her eyes widened, her hand shaking as she reached inside and pulled out a prescription bottle.

"Someone left that?" he asked, watching her face. "What are they?"

"Painkillers." And he suspected she'd like to take them to kill some of her pain. Was that how she'd survived on the streets? Drugs?

He'd only lived a short time where she'd been living—on the streets. He couldn't imagine what she'd seen, what she'd had to do…to survive.

But she put back that brown bottle and reached for another. "Here's some peroxide, but there are no cotton swabs."

"I noticed a roll of paper towels left on the kitchen counter," he said. "You could use that."

She looked at the medicine cabinet, her face reflected back in the tarnished mirror, then she headed out of the room. Ty stood up, opened the cabinet door and picked up the prescription bottle that had held her attention. He popped off the cap and held the bottle over the toilet.

He had to flush them. He needed her lucid. He couldn't bring her back to her sisters out of her mind on drugs.

"I won't be," she spoke eerily to his thoughts,

her voice soft as she walked up behind him. She reached around him and grabbed the bottle. "I stopped using drugs and alcohol…."

He didn't have to be able to read her mind to know that the pills tempted her, that alcohol probably would, too. He didn't let go of the bottle. He wouldn't let her hurt herself again.

"I don't need them," she assured him. "But *you* might for your head. It's Vicodin."

"Irina…"

"You've asked me to trust you," she said. "You need to trust me."

More than once he'd requested her trust, and she'd given it. Trust didn't come easily for Ty.

"You think it comes easy for *me?*" she asked. "I don't even trust myself."

"Then how can you expect me to?" he asked, tugging the bottle out of her hand.

"I can't." She dropped the paper towel in the sink and walked into the bedroom. The springs creaked as she settled onto the mattress. "We're going to have to share this bed."

He put the prescription bottle back in the cabinet with the peroxide. His head was fine; it was his heart that beat crazily.

"I'll sleep on the floor," he said as he joined her in the bedroom.

She shook her head, holding her arms up to him. "No. Please, Ty, I need you."

Chapter 5

Despite the sunshine burning through the pickup's windshield, Irina shivered, as chilled as she'd been back in the alley. Not because of the wind whistling through the back window but because Ty's arms weren't around her like he'd held her the night before. All night.

"I need to bring you to your sisters," Ty said even though he steered his silver pickup truck away from downtown Barrett—where she assumed David's penthouse was—heading toward the suburbs instead.

Irina drew in a deep breath, wondering if he

wanted to bring her to her sisters for their sake or his. Did he just want to get rid of her? She couldn't blame him if he did.

"I *can't* meet them," Irina insisted as she had the night before, "not until I find the charm." *If* she was able to find it, even with his help. What the hell had she done with it? "I can't bring them *nothing.*"

"You're not bringing them nothing," he argued. "All they want is you."

They didn't know her anymore; she wasn't the child she'd once been, their sweet baby sister. They couldn't love her, they just needed her charm.

"Liar," she called him as she peered through her lashes at him.

His mouth lifted into that lopsided grin. "Man, you must be impossible to…"

"Lie to?" she persisted, her nerves easing a bit as they bantered. The seat belt tightened across her chest as she shifted around, lifting her legs under her. She wore crisp new jeans and a warm chenille sweater—clothes Ty had picked up for her that morning, when he'd left her sleeping in the bed they'd shared and gone out without her, leaving her alone.

With the prescription bottle in the cabinet. Even though it hadn't been easy for him, he'd trusted her. And even though it had not been easy for her, she hadn't violated his trust. Yet.

"You'd be impossible to have a relationship with," he said, then hastened to add, "I mean, the poor slob you date wouldn't stand a chance—"

"Of lying and cheating on me," she interrupted, her voice hardening with a flare of bitterness. "No, he wouldn't." Pain flickered through her, the hurts so old she'd nearly forgotten, as she had so many other parts of her past.

"I didn't mean—" He sighed. "I wasn't talking about infidelity, about lying. It's just that sometimes it's better that *no one* know what you're thinking."

The resentment rolling through her now was his. He hated that she knew things about him that no one else knew, the full extent of his pain. Of his fear.

But he was right. Maybe she'd have been happier if she didn't know everything. None of her few relationships had lasted. No matter what pretty lies the men in her life had told, she'd always known what they'd really thought, how they'd really felt. And so she'd always been disillusioned. Until last night. Until she'd lain in his arms all through the night.

He'd just held her, probably because she'd begged him to, because she'd been so weary of being alone. They'd slept with their clothes on, and even with the memory of their kiss burning their minds and their lips, they hadn't sought anything more than warmth from each other. Ty had lain flat on his back on the bare mattress, and Irina had used his chest as a pillow, listening to his heart beat slow and hard beneath her cheek. Despite the short time they'd known each other, they'd never felt like strangers.

Because of the first time they'd met, so many years ago, they had a special bond. She knew Ty resented that, too.

No one should know what you're feeling. No one should have to feel it, too.

Even though she heard his thought, she couldn't fathom what he was feeling. At the moment, she couldn't feel anything but her own apprehension and fear. Last night all she'd felt was his. While his arms around her had given her comfort through the night, maybe he'd found some, too. Because he'd slept in the house where he'd lived nothing but nightmares.

"What are *you* thinking?" he asked.

She couldn't think about him, about how they shared a memory of a battered kid in a hospital, of a little girl begging him not to die. As she'd come to his aid so many years ago, he'd come to hers. Fate again?

She couldn't use his strength; she had to bolster

her own. She had to take care of herself instead of relying on him. She drew in a deep breath.

"I'm thinking that I haven't been home in a long time." She sighed. "That they probably won't be happy to see me."

He lifted that scarred brow in a silent question. He couldn't read her thoughts, but he must have guessed she hadn't told him the entire truth. Police instincts or their connection again? "Irina—"

"Heather," she corrected him.

"What?"

"*They* want Heather," she said, her stomach churning with nerves. She couldn't summon strength when the thought of returning "home" resurrected her every insecurity. "They want nothing to do with Irina Cooper."

"Who's Heather?"

"Me. Since the adoption." Something that never would have happened if her biological mother hadn't given her up, hadn't signed off her parental rights.

She pushed aside the twinge of regret that she and Ty hadn't made love the night before; it was better that they hadn't. If she got involved any deeper with him, she'd only get hurt. She might have a connection to Ty, forged in the past, but like everyone else from her past, she knew he could never love her. No matter what they'd called her, no one—at least no adult—had ever really loved Irina Cooper. Her sisters might have as kids.

"The adoption, the name change," he said, "that's why we couldn't find you."

"That's why." She sighed again, a catchy little expulsion of air. "They told me I was born Heather Bowers. That I had no sisters. No family before them."

"You weren't a baby anymore," he said. "You had to have known the truth."

She jerked her chin up and down in a rough nod. "I knew the truth."

"But still, that must have confused you," he said, his raspy voice soft with sympathy, "to have adults lying to you. To be told you weren't who you'd always been."

Her breath shuddered out. "Yeah, so for a while, for a long time, I wasn't who I'd always been. I tried to be Heather for them."

"To make them happy."

She nodded. But she hadn't made them happy. She'd brought them nothing but misery.

"Why didn't they adopt a baby," he asked, "since they wanted someone who wouldn't remember her life before the adoption?"

"They wanted a baby," she said, recounting their thoughts, their disappointment in her. "But they were older. My adoptive father, Richard, had already had a heart attack before they got me. They'd been denied a baby but were allowed to adopt an older child."

"They shouldn't have been allowed to adopt at all," Ty said as he shook his head, his jaw taut and even darker with stubble. A few things had been left in the house—the bed, some toiletries, but no razor. He could have picked up one when he'd bought her clothes, but he'd thought first of her needs and not of his. Her heart shifted in her chest, as if moving in his direction.

She drew a deep breath, focusing on the Bowers instead of Ty and her growing feelings for him. Like so much of her life, they couldn't be real, based only on gratitude and fear. Nothing more. Nothing lasting.

"The Bowers are good people," she defended. "They really, really tried to love me."

Unlike Ty's father, who'd only really tried to kill him. His pain filtered through hers, so much more intense than anything she'd ever personally felt. He'd been abused both physically and emotionally. Would the man that the boy had become be able to love when he'd never really been loved?

She'd thought she'd known love, long ago, when she'd been with her mother and her sisters. But if her mother had loved her, why had she let her go?

Her sisters, although children themselves, had loved her. She remembered their arms around her, protectively, the way Ty had held her through the night. They didn't know her now; they couldn't love her anymore. But she owed them for the affection they'd once given her.

"I hope I left it at the Bowersers'," she said. And hadn't sold it, as she'd sold so many other things. But she'd never sold herself. She'd not given her body freely, not even in those few relationships she'd had. Because she'd never been shown much affection, she didn't know how to show it to others, how to be physically close to someone. Until Ty, until she'd spent the night in his arms wishing for more.

But was she just using him as a distraction, the way she'd used the drugs and alcohol?

"You're sure you remember where they live?" he asked.

She nodded. "I have a lot of blanks in my memory." Erased either by the alcohol or the trauma of the thoughts she'd heard, the pain she'd felt. "But I remember...."

"You don't sound like you want to go back there."

She didn't have a choice. "I have to find the charm...for my sisters."

"What do you know about them?" he asked, obviously not referring only to memories but to what she'd gleaned through her ability to read minds.

"I've heard Ariel's and Elena's thoughts," she admitted, "or conversations. I wasn't sure who they were...." When she'd been out of her mind. She hadn't been sure what was real or not during that time. She'd heard so many horrible things, had felt so much pain and suffering. "I know they think the charms will stop the witch hunt."

She turned to him, but he stared ahead at the road. He hadn't looked at her since last night, since she'd stepped inside the past he'd thought he'd buried so deep...with his father.

"Do you think the charms will stop it?" she asked him. His opinion mattered to her—too much. A little bubble of relief lifted her heart; she wasn't using him.

He shrugged his shoulders, so broad they strained the cotton of his dark blue T-shirt. "I've been struggling with the whole thing. The three-hundred-and-fifty-year-old vendetta."

"I'm not sure how much I remember of it. I know Mama told us…"

"A story. How her ancestor, Myra Durikken, had a vision of lightning starting a fire that burned down the McGregor family's house. How she warned them, but the men were gone and the women, too afraid to believe her, died in the fire she foretold." His voice hardened as he continued, "And Eli McGregor returned to find his family dead and blamed the witch."

Breathless, as she'd been when Mama had shared the legend twenty years ago, she asked, "Was she a witch?"

He shrugged again. "She used herbs and secret potions to heal people. She had special powers."

"She was a witch," Irina confirmed, pride filling her instead of fear. Her ancestor had healed people; she had used her powers to help, not harm.

"So Eli avenged his family by burning Myra at the stake. But not for what she did. We have his journal. We know that he did it to retrieve the charms she used to heal him when years before he was struck by lightning. I guess she forged the charms of the earth where the lightning struck it. But they look like pewter…."

From the way he filled her in, his voice heavy with doubt, it was apparent that he struggled to believe. Irina could understand his reluctance to accept the legend as truth; she'd struggled so long with whether or not to believe.

"From his journal we learned Eli is actually the one who called forth the lightning to kill his family," Ty continued. "Then he used their deaths as an excuse to kill her. Since the lightning strike, he'd had some powers of his own, but he wanted hers. He wanted her charms, too."

"*He* was a witch?"

Ty's broad shoulders lifted in another shrug. "Or wizard. I don't know. He was a lunatic, completely out of his mind—like Donovan Roarke, his descendent."

"There were other McGregor descendents," she said. There had to have been.

"Your sister Elena is half McGregor. Her grandmother is the reason your mother lost her children. She swore out a complaint against her so she could give Elena to her son. After he died, she found Roarke and gave him the journal."

"She started up the witch hunt again? She wanted him to kill us?" Now she understood why sometimes, when she'd been inside Elena's head, guilt and regret had weighed so heavily on her heart that it had stolen away her breath.

"Thora Jones, Elena's grandmother, wanted the charms. Like Eli, like your sisters, she believed they had special powers."

"*Wanted?* Past tense? She doesn't anymore?"

"She's dead," he said. "Roarke killed her."

"He's killed a lot of people." And she'd heard all their pleas for mercy and their cries of pain, mingled together, indistinguishable from one another. Except the one that had begun it all—her mother's.

And…

"He hurt *you*," she said. She recalled his limp from when he'd walked through the rooms of his old house last night. She hadn't noticed it when Roarke had been chasing them, but it must have hurt him. He'd moved stiffly this morning, his face tense with pain.

"I fell through a staircase in an old church," he said, his raspy voice thick with self-disgust, "where he'd begun a cult, trying to get other people to help him on his witch hunt. My friend David—your sister Ariel's fiancé—infiltrated the cult."

But Roarke had gotten away from them. Ty's frustration churned in her stomach; he blamed himself. She reached across the seat, settling her hand on his thigh. Muscles bunched beneath her palm. "We'll stop him."

If she could find her charm…

Why had she lost such an important part of her past, of her heritage? But then, she shouldn't be surprised; she'd lost herself, too. She hoped the charm wouldn't be as hard to find.

"Turn here," she directed, gesturing toward the

sign for the cul-de-sac on which she'd grown up. "It's the third house on the left."

Ty pulled the truck to the curb in front of the proud Victorian. Yellow paint brightened the clapboard siding, and the windows gleamed. Cora and Richard Bowers took great pride in their home, in the gingerbread trim and colorful gardens.

They'd taken more pride in their house than their daughter. But she couldn't blame them. She hadn't given them much of which to be proud. During that time in her teens and again recently, she'd been a mess. She'd stolen from them, using the money for booze and drugs. She drew in a breath, bracing herself for an ugly confrontation.

Not that any harsh words would be spoken. They might not speak to her at all, just freeze her out with their cold disapproval.

"They're good people," she said again, more to convince herself than Ty.

"Irina…"

"Don't call me Irina in there, in front of them," she cautioned him, her stomach flipping as her nerves increased. What would the Bowerses think of Ty? Would they sense the connection between them and figure they were involved?

"I *can't* call you Heather," he said, his voice sharp with disapproval for the Bowerses.

The feeling would undoubtedly be mutual if they knew Ty had been suspended from his job, that he'd broken her out of a psychiatric ward. "Maybe you should wait here."

He reached down, closing his hand over hers on his thigh. She hadn't known it was still there; she'd never needed to touch someone the way she needed to touch Ty. But then, she'd gone so long alone that perhaps she just needed to touch *someone*. Anyone.

Her stomach twisted at the thought. She'd been with the wrong men before; she wouldn't be crazy enough to give herself away again. Not unless there were feelings—real feelings—involved and not just desperation and loneliness.

"You're not going in there alone," he insisted. But his unspoken thought told her more than his words. *You didn't let me be alone last night. In that hell.*

"It wasn't hell growing up here," she tried to convince him.

At least it wouldn't have been hell if she'd fit in. She reached for the door handle. She had to find the charm. Hopefully she'd left it here, among the other mementos of her childhood. And hopefully Cora and Richard hadn't found and discarded it.

Ty met her on the sidewalk and took her hand in his again as they walked up the front steps. She turned a newel post on the railing and pulled out the hide-away key. Maybe she should have knocked instead, but this was the house where she'd grown up. Even though she'd never really been part of the family, she would have felt silly ringing the bell. The key turned easily in the lock.

Surprise flickered through her that they hadn't changed the locks, that they hadn't at least removed the hide-away key. Maybe they cared about and trusted her more than she'd realized, more than she deserved. The mahogany door creaked open.

Crime-scene tape. The thought ran through Ty's mind as he pulled a piece of yellow from the doorjamb. "Irina, don't…."

But she'd already stepped across the threshold. The parquet flooring, usually bright with polish, had been tramped dull with dusty footprints.

"Cora won't like this," she murmured, then she walked into the parlor. Her heart slammed against her ribs as fear and regret flowed through her.

Some of those screams she'd heard unjumbled. She recognized the agonized cry of her adoptive father. The terrorized scream of her adoptive mother. The blood sprayed on the wall behind the Victorian fainting couch foretold where they'd died. And Irina knew how and why.

Because of her. Because Donovan Roarke had been convinced they knew where she was, that they'd been protecting her by not revealing her location.

She runs away, she always has, Richard Bowers had claimed, swallowing nervously against the knife held tight to his throat. *We don't know where she is.*

She winced as the blade cut and his guttural cry tore from his slashed throat. "Noooo!" Irina's cry echoed Cora's as she'd watched her beloved husband die. She'd been helpless to save him. Or herself. In that last minute, before Roarke had killed her, she'd hated Irina. Not him. She'd hated the child they'd adopted for bringing such evil into their perfect home, into their perfect, too-short lives.

Irina dropped to her knees, pain and hatred crashing over her. Strong arms wrapped around her, pulling her up, turning her so that her tears fell against a hard chest, soaked into a dark T-shirt. Ty's hands tunneled into her hair, clasping her head against his shoulder. "Shh…"

She choked back the sobs strangling her. "I—I—I kn-kn-know what happened."

"Roarke," Ty said, not needing to read her mind. "Somehow the bastard did what we weren't able to. He got into your sealed adoption record."

"He tortured them to find out where I was." A sob smothered her, but she fought against the sorrow and regret. "They didn't know where I was." Hell, she hadn't known. They shouldn't have had to suffer any more over her. "I'm so sorry...."

"It wasn't your fault. None of this is your fault," he insisted, his arms tightening around her, holding her closer as if trying to absorb her pain. "Donovan Roarke is insane."

As she'd thought she was. "They didn't deserve this...." They hadn't deserved her. If only they had been able to adopt that perfect child they'd wanted instead of her, Richard and Cora Bowers would still be alive.

"Let's get you out of here," Ty said, turning her toward the foyer, away from the room splattered with her adoptive parents' blood.

She shook her head and drew in a deep breath. "No, we came for the charm. We have to find it."

"I'll search," he said, obviously no more willing to leave without the charm than she was. "I know what it looks like."

And she didn't remember the charm that was such an important part of her heritage, of her identity. She glanced again toward the blood-spatter stains, more brown than red now against the pearly pink walls. The charm was also her salvation, if she remembered the legend correctly. Myra Durikken had given her daughter the charms to keep her safe as well as to make her remember who and what she was; Myra Cooper, Irina's mother, had had the same intention when she'd bestowed the charms on her daughters.

Irina lifted her chin and retreated from his arms, pulling herself together. For so long she'd been alone, with only herself to rely on. She'd failed herself a couple times before, but she wouldn't again. "I know my hiding places."

"We'll both look," he said.

They weren't the only ones who'd searched the house. They found every drawer upended, all the rooms ransacked. Pillows and mattresses and old stuffed animals were slashed, stuffing spilling from them. His rage hung yet in the air, as heavy as the scent of death that filled the closed-up house.

"What if he's found it?" she asked as they tore apart the upstairs turret room where she used to sleep—when she'd been able to sleep without the thoughts of others rolling through her mind, disrupting her dreams.

Now she knew some of those thoughts had been Ty's. Their connection had remained throughout the years, sometimes tenuous and almost forgotten, and other times crystal clear. She remembered the struggle, his rage as he'd fought with the father of that little girl. She was the one he thought he'd failed, because he'd gotten to her house too late to save her.

"Ty…"

"Hello?" called out a voice from the entrance.

Ty pressed a finger to his lips and headed toward the stairs. "Can I help you?" he asked, his footsteps clunking against the hardwood steps. "I'm Officer McIntyre."

The lie—that was what he thought it—cost him some of the integrity in which he'd taken such pride. She cost him.

She sat back and gazed around her childhood room, the frothy pink roses that covered the walls, the ceiling as pearly pink as the parlor walls. The carpet, plush beneath her knees, was rose-colored.

She'd never fit in here, in this room, this house, this neighborhood. This had never really been her life. No wonder there was so much of it she struggled to remember.

"I'm Mrs. Canaberry," a female voice answered. The busybody from across the street. "I saw you and a woman go inside and thought…"

"Detective Howard."

"Is she the woman? She looked like…"

"Who?" Ty's question was short and direct.

Irina could imagine what kind of officer he'd been. A good one. Her shoulders bowed, guilt weighing heavy on them. Because of her, he'd never serve again.

"The woman looked like the Bowerses' daughter," she said, her voice rising with salacious excitement. "You know, the one the police think did this horrible thing."

Irina's breath caught. The police thought *she* had done this. Panic rose, bringing a cry to her lips. But she pressed her hand against her mouth to hold it in.

"She's crazy, you know," the busybody continued to gossip. "Has been since the day they adopted her. I don't know why they didn't give her back. She broke their hearts, stealing from them, running away, acting crazy. If only they had given her back…"

They'd be alive. Mrs. Canaberry might have been a gossip, but she wasn't wrong.

Irina drew in a breath, summoning that inner strength into which she'd tapped so seldom she hadn't realized how deep it ran. She was stronger— and definitely saner—than she'd ever realized.

"Where is she?" the woman asked.

"Who?" Ty shot back at her.

"Your Detective Howard."

"She had to go to another call." His retort was as fast as his earlier question.

"I didn't see her leave."

"She went out the back way," he lied, so easily. "Her car was in the driveway."

"I never saw—"

Irina couldn't hear the rest of what she said or what Ty murmured in that deep, raspy voice of his. She only heard the click of the door as he showed her out. Then the uneven thump of his feet on the stairs as he limped up to her.

"We have to get out of here," she said, speaking his thought.

"She's going in now to use the phone. To check on my story," he said, glancing out the curved front windows to the heavyset woman rushing across the street to her bungalow.

"Maybe you can read minds, too," she mused.

"Just people. Occupational hazard," he quipped, his voice wistful.

"You gave her your real name," she realized, anxiety pressing on her heart.

"She'd already taken down my plate number," he said. "She'd know."

He'd given up so much for her. His job. His integrity.

"The charm's not here," she said with one last

wistful sigh as she glanced around the room of her youth. She obviously hadn't lived here, in this room of dainty flowers and delicate furniture, as an adult. But where had she lived? Her head pounded as she tried to remember.

Ty's hand closed over her arm, tugging her toward the stairs. "Come on," he said. "We have to leave before the police get here."

He'd once been one of them. Because of her, because of what he'd already done for her, he never would be again. But his career was the least of her worries for Ty. She was more concerned for his life.

Roarke was intent on killing him. And only the charm she couldn't find could stop the madman.

The flames sprang up around him, smoke rising, burning his eyes as the heat burned his flesh. Through the smoke he caught sight of the witches, their hair concealed by hoods, their faces shadowed but for their smiling red mouths. They laughed at him, their laughter rising above the crackle and roar of the fire.

They'd beaten him, so much more powerful than he could have ever been. Now he would never be—

He jerked awake, his eyes opening to the water-stained ceiling. Then he cringed against the light as his head pounded. The tumor was growing; it was almost as if he could feel it invading his head…the way the witch had. In the alley, she'd claimed to read his mind.

Was that her power? If so, she was more dangerous than the others. But then killing her would probably make him even more powerful than if he killed one of her sisters or her niece.

The police scanner, sitting on the scratched table beside the bed, screeched out an APB for one Tyler McIntyre, former police officer of Barrett, wanted for questioning in the escape of a mental patient at Barrett Community Hospital and a subsequent shooting. He had just been sighted at the crime scene of the unsolved murders of Richard and Cora Bowers. A woman matching the description of the escaped mental patient accompanied him.

The radio crackled as other officers reported they'd check out the scene, reading back their call numbers and the street address.

A warning emanated from the scanner: "McIntyre should be considered armed and dangerous."

Roarke rolled over on the thin mattress on which he lay. Then he flung one of the heavy pillows across the room, where it struck the wall and fell to a heap on the floor. Dust motes rose from the dilapidated mess. The hotel was a dump. But it took cash, untraceable to him. And it was close to McIntyre's house. But the cop hadn't returned there last night. Nor had he gone to either of the witches.

Where had he taken the dark-haired one? Besides her adoptive parents' house.

Roarke could rush over there, too. But McIntyre would be gone before the police got there, let alone Roarke. He had to get ahead of McIntyre instead of chasing behind him.

He'd made a point of finding out everything he could about the witches and the men who cared about them. His head pounded as he sat up and reached for his briefcase. Inside was a file on each of them: Elena Jones-Phillips; her daughter, Stacia; her boyfriend, the CEO Joseph Dolce; Ariel Cooper; her fiancé, the computer mogul David Koster and his friend, the cop Ty McIntyre. Until now, Donovan hadn't been too concerned about McIntyre. The suspended cop hadn't had the vested interest of the others. He hadn't loved one of the witches; he'd only been doing a favor for a friend.

When had it become something more? When had Irina Cooper become something more to him?

She must have bewitched him, the way the other women had bewitched the powerful men who were devoted to them. She'd condemned Ty McIntyre to death.

He pulled out McIntyre's file. This was what he was best at—finding people, learning all their dirty secrets. His file on McIntyre would grow…until he found him.

And killed him.

Chapter 6

"God, Ty, do you have any idea what the hell you're doing?" David's voice, sharp with anger, vibrated through the phone.

What the hell *was* he doing? Giving up his freedom? That was what David had warned him about last night.

But instead of seeing prison bars, Ty saw *her* as he peered through the doorway to where Irina sat on the one bed in the house, the one they'd shared last night. Even though the mattress was lumpy, it was soft. Not that he'd gotten much sleep with her clinging to him, her soft body pressed against his. The memory of their kiss had haunted him, embedded in his mind and on his lips.

He'd struggled all night against the urge to lift her head from his chest and press his lips to hers again, to run his hands over her soft, warm body. But he couldn't take advantage of her then…and especially not now, when he had a better understanding of what she'd endured.

"Bring her here," David commanded. He was used to bossing around his employees; sometimes he forgot Ty wasn't one of them. Even before his suspension, David had offered him a job. Head of security. This or that title, ridiculous amounts of money that any man would be a fool to turn down.

Ty was a fool.

He stopped pacing around the worn linoleum kitchen floor and turned again to study Irina through the bedroom doorway. She sat in the middle of the bare mattress, her knees drawn up against her chest, her arms wrapped around them, holding herself…when he should be holding her instead.

And now, what was he doing? He was arguing with a friend, risking one of the few relationships he'd allowed himself. But what David didn't know was that Ty didn't need his money. Ty didn't need anything or anyone. At least he hadn't…until he'd spent the night in her arms.

Now he didn't know what he needed.

"Ty!" David shouted. "What the hell's wrong with you? You gotta know you're going to go to jail."

He couldn't resist taunting his friend. "Only if they catch me."

"Damn it, Ty," David raged. "A former police officer would never survive in prison. You need to come here right now. I'll call a lawyer I know."

David Koster was used to getting what he wanted, to having people ask how high when he told them to jump. But after all the years they'd known each other, he should have realized Ty wasn't a jumper.

His sigh rattled the phone and echoed in his own ear. "I'm not bringing her to the penthouse."

"Why the *hell* not?"

"She doesn't want to meet her sisters yet," Ty said, his voice lowered although it didn't matter whether he spoke softly or not at all. She would still know what he said; she knew his every thought. His muscles tensed, but he couldn't fight her. He couldn't keep her out, no matter how hard he tried.

And he wasn't going to force her to do anything she wasn't ready to do. She'd been through too much: today, seeing where and how her adoptive parents had died, and the past few months she'd spent living on the street, lost inside her own head. Actually, knowing now the way her adoptive parents had treated her, *none* of her life had been easy.

David's sigh shuddered through the phone. "How am I supposed to tell Ariel that?" He lowered *his* voice. "How am I supposed to tell her that her little sister doesn't want to meet her?"

Regret pressed on Ty's heart. He didn't want to hurt Ariel or her sister. But he wanted to hurt Irina even less.

"It's not that she doesn't want to see Ariel and Elena," Ty defended. He understood her. Maybe he *could* get inside her head a little, the way he had that one time so long ago. "She doesn't feel that she *can* meet them until she finds her charm."

"Screw the charm!" Like Ty, David didn't always know what to believe about the vendetta. Would having all three charms, all three sisters together, stop the witch hunt, as they believed?

Ty didn't know. But Irina believed, and that was enough for him. "She's trying to remember where she lived after she moved out of her adoptive parents' house."

"God, what all is wrong with her?" David asked with little sympathy for the weak. He was too strong to understand weakness; Ariel was his only one. For a while she had been Ty's, too.

David recounted what he knew about Irina. "She was homeless, then picked up off the street and committed to a psych ward. She can't remember—"

Ty interrupted him, his defense of Irina sharpening his voice. "She's been through a lot."

She'd endured everything all of Roarke's victims had been through. Only a few of them had lived. So with each of those who had died, a piece of Irina had died, too…until she'd had so little left of herself.

"That's why she needs her sisters," David maintained, "for support. *They* are the only ones who can truly understand what she's been going through."

And Ty couldn't? He couldn't give her the support and understanding she needed? Hell, maybe he couldn't. He'd never been good at dealing with the victims of crime, only the suspects.

"Bring her here." David ended the call, as if he believed Ty wouldn't dare disobey his command.

How could they have been friends so long and David still know him so little? Because Ty hadn't let him. He hadn't let anyone know him. Not even Irina, but somehow she'd still managed to crawl into his head.

His heart shifted in his chest, lurching as emotion flooded it. Had she crawled into his heart, too? He dropped his cell phone onto the chipped

laminate counter and walked into the bedroom
where she'd been alone too long.

"He's wrong," she said, her voice a soft whisper
as she gazed up at him with luminescent eyes.

Ty nodded as he admitted his brilliant friend's
many failings. "He often is." But he loved him
like a brother.

Her mouth lifted in a faint smile. "About *me*.
He's wrong about me."

"I know," Ty agreed. "You're not crazy."

David hadn't said it, but Ty'd known the man
so long he could imagine what he was thinking.
David didn't understand how much Irina had
suffered for the sins of others, of Eli McGregor
and Donovan Roarke.

"No, that's not what I'm referring to." Her
delicate throat moved as she swallowed hard. "I
don't need *just* my sisters."

"You do need them—"

"Yes, but I need you, too." She raised her hand
and held it out to him, saying and doing the same
thing she'd done the night before.

But somehow he suspected she wanted him to
do more than just hold her the way he had last
night. His heart beat fast and hard, hammering
against his ribs. He knew he should walk away
while he still could. But instead he walked closer

to the bed and took her hand, enfolding it in his. Despite being so slim and fragile-looking, she was strong. She tugged him down onto the mattress next to her.

"I need *you*, Ty," she said again, her voice filled with desire.

"Irina…"

She gazed up at him, studying him through her lashes. "I know you don't need anyone—or you don't want to—but…"

"Irina, I can't take advantage—"

She pressed her fingers against his lips. "You're not taking advantage of me." She drew in a deep breath, then added, "Unless you're using me—"

Her fingers stroked his lips as he interrupted her. "I won't use you. I don't want to do anything that will hurt you."

"You're not going to hurt me…unless you're using me as a consolation prize for my sister."

"What are you talking about?"

"Ariel. We need to talk about Ariel." Her dark eyes shimmered with emotion, with longing. For her sisters or for him?

"She's anxious to see you—"

Her fingers slid from his lips as she shook her head. "Not about Ariel and me, about Ariel and you."

"There's nothing to talk about," he insisted.

He'd once had feelings for Ariel. She was so beautiful, so sweet, a man would have to be dead to *not*
react to her.

But then he'd realized that what he'd felt for her
wasn't real; it didn't compare to her love for David
and David's love for her. "We're just friends."

"Now."

"Always." For a brief time he'd wanted more,
but he and Ariel weren't meant to be.

They weren't fated to be together the way he
feared he and Irina might be. He shook his head,
trying to clear it. He didn't believe in fate. A man
made his own. He took care of himself…and those
he cared about.

"Ty." Still holding his hand, she threaded her
fingers through his, binding them together. "Stop
fighting it."

Fate? Had she read his mind again?

"Stop fighting *me*," she clarified.

"I'm trying to do the right thing here," he said
as his conscience battled his desire. His chest
strained with each ragged breath he took. "I'm
trying not to take advantage of you. You're a—"

"Mess," she interrupted him. "I don't have
my life together. Yet. But I know who I am. And
I know what you are. An honorable man, Ty
McIntyre. But today, tonight, whatever it is…"

The last light of day penetrated the tattered shade, casting light like confetti across the scarred hardwood floor. "We need each other."

She pulled her hand from his and reached for the hem of her sweater—the one he'd bought for her this morning, instinctively knowing her size and that orange was her favorite color. When she'd opened the bag of clothes, she'd confirmed his guesses as accurate.

He swallowed hard as she lifted the sweater. He'd undressed her last night, in the hospital, but he hadn't been able to see her. He'd only felt the silky softness of her skin as he'd untied her hospital gown and pulled the scrubs over her head. Now she pulled off the chenille sweater, her hair tangling around her shoulders as she pulled her head free. Then she dropped the sweater onto the floor. Now he could appreciate her beauty: the honey glow of her skin, the dark areolae of her nipples, the fullness of her rounded breasts. His hands shaking, he reached for her.

But instead of touching her body, he touched her face, gliding his fingertips along the curve of her cheek. "Are you sure?"

She smiled, her dark eyes brightening. "For the first time in a long time, yes. I'm sure of what I want. I want you, Ty. I *need* you."

He could deny her and himself no longer. He tipped up her chin and settled his mouth onto hers, sipping from her lips, sliding his tongue into her honey sweetness. Her tongue met his shyly, tasting and retreating. Then her teeth nipped, both playful and bold.

His erection pressed against the fly of his jeans, throbbing with desire, painful in intensity. "Irina…"

"You don't have to be gentle," she murmured against his mouth before he had even formed the thought, let alone spoken it.

He didn't like that she knew everything he thought, everything he felt, but for the moment he didn't care…he didn't care about anything but her. About giving her the reprieve she needed from all the trauma she'd endured. He brushed his fingers through her hair, pushing the tangle of long, brown curls from her bare shoulders. Then his fingertips skimmed across her shoulders, tracing the delicate curve of her collarbone, then lower.

Her breath caught, then shuddered out between her lips, brushing over his mouth as he took one of her breasts in his hand. The heavy weight filled his palm, the skin silky-soft and warm. He stroked his thumb across the nipple, which hardened and pushed against the callused pad. Back and forth he stroked while she gnawed her bottom lip and whimpered his name. "Ty, Ty…"

Then he replaced his thumb with his mouth, tugging at the turgid point with his lips before laving the sensitive peak with his tongue. Her fingers tunneled through his hair, first tugging him away then pulling him closer.

She lifted up from the bed, her hips thrusting against his. Even through their jeans he felt the rush of heat as she came, shuddering in the aftermath of her climax. Her voice breathy with surprise and embarrassment, she murmured, "Ty, I never…you just…"

"Shh…" he said, his voice muffled against her breast. He didn't want her to feel shame; he didn't want her to feel anything but pleasure. He reached between them, unsnapped her jeans and dragged down the zipper until he could push his fingers through her moist curls, through the slick wetness of her desire.

"I have to taste you," he said, his heart beating violently against his ribs as his body throbbed. But he wasn't worried about his own satisfaction; all that mattered was hers. He stripped the denim off her legs, sliding his palms along her soft thighs and contoured calves.

She writhed on the bed, thrashing her head

against the hard, flat pillow he'd found in a closet last night. He blew his breath along her skin, raising goose bumps on the silky flesh. Then he pressed delicate kisses along her calves, her thighs, the curve of her hip. When his mouth settled between her legs, she reached for the brass rails, wrapping her hands around them. He lapped at her wetness, her sweetness filling his senses. He pushed his tongue into her, deep into her heat.

Her thighs parted in surrender as she gave herself up to the passion, to the pleasure he gave her with his mouth and with his fingers stroking over her breasts, plucking at her nipples. He drove her up and over the edge of sanity. She sobbed into the pillow, writhing around as orgasm after orgasm bubbled from her.

He'd never given anyone so much pleasure, had never felt so much himself even though he had yet to remove a stitch of clothing. As if just realizing he was fully dressed, she lurched up from the mattress and launched herself at him. She lifted up his T-shirt, pulling it over his chest, stopping only to slide her mouth over his pecs.

"Ty, you're so gorgeous…so perfect…." she murmured between pants for breath as she tugged the shirt over his head and tossed it onto the floor.

Did she not see the scars, both old and new, that

had stopped so many other women, that had had them sucking in their breath with surprise, their eyes widening with fear?

"I'm not afraid of you, Ty," she murmured as she slid her mouth over his chest, flicking her tongue over each old cigarette burn as if it to wash it away.

"Maybe you should be." She more than anyone else, because she tested his control, which threatened to snap with each touch of her tongue, each brush of her fingertips against his skin. He sucked in a breath when she ran her hand up his side, over the ridge along his ribs.

"Ty…" She gazed up at him, her dark eyes shimmering with tears.

"Don't," he warned her. He'd rather she fear than pity him. "Don't…"

She lifted her chin and tossed her head with pride, but her words confirmed it was in him, not in herself. "You're a warrior, Ty McIntyre. The strongest man I've ever known."

His heart shifted, moved by her words, by her pride. Before he could pull her close, her hands closed over the snap of his jeans. He caught her wrists, not pulling her away, just holding her still…as he listened.

To knocking. Something pounding against

something. Then music pealed out, the theme from *Mission: Impossible*. His phone, first vibrating against the counter, then ringing. Obviously David had realized Ty wasn't jumping.

"Ignore it," she implored him. She unsnapped his jeans, then pushed her fingers inside his waistband, rubbing them over the tip of his penis, which strained his shorts and the zipper of his jeans.

His breath shuddered out. He wasn't jumping for David. But for her, he'd do anything....

Take any risk.

"Irina..."

"I want you, Ty. I *need* you." Her trembling fingers fumbled with the tab for his zipper.

So he didn't come too soon, he stood up and shucked the jeans himself, along with his tennis shoes and socks. But then he reached down to pull his wallet out of the back pocket and a condom from his wallet.

"What a Boy Scout," she praised him as he rolled on the rubber. She watched him, her eyes molten with desire. "Always prepared..."

"No. I could have never prepared for you," he insisted. He'd had no idea anyone like her existed. Even in heaven.

"Oh, Ty," she murmured, her hands sliding over

his chest again, then down his stomach to his penis throbbing inside its latex sheath.

"Take it off," she pleaded. "Let me do to you what you did to—"

"No. I want *you*. Now." He pushed her back onto the mattress. But instead of burying himself inside her the way his body demanded as it shook with desire, he struggled for control. She deserved more, so much more. So he touched her again, sliding his fingers inside her, making sure she was still wet and ready for him.

She shuddered and convulsed around his hand, weeping his name. "Ty…"

He'd never known anyone as responsive as she was, as passionate. He kissed her, nipping at her full bottom lip, sucking it into his mouth. Her lips parted for his tongue, pulling him in. She moaned and whimpered, panting when he finally broke the kiss. Then he leaned over and closed his lips around her nipple, tugging at the sensitive point until she writhed beneath him.

When he could stand her moans and cries no longer, he pulled back, spread her thighs and buried himself inside her heat. Her muscles closed around him, pulling him deep, holding him tight, stroking him as she came again and again.

His control snapped, and he thrust into her heat

over and over, desire buzzing in his head, roaring in his ears…until the only thing he heard was his own guttural cry of release as his orgasm drained out of him and he collapsed in her arms.

Irina snuggled tight against Ty's bare chest, running her fingertips over the scars that marred and puckered his skin. Her warrior, battered but unbreakable. He had so much strength she both admired and envied.

Last night, tired of being alone, she'd appreciated his closeness. Tonight, with no clothes to separate skin from skin, she reveled in being next to him, in remembering what it had felt like to be a part of him. Her blood hummed, denying her the sleep he slept, of the dead. Or the extremely satisfied. After he'd cleaned up, they'd made love again…in the old shower, under the spurts of lukewarm water. Yet with their passion, the mirrors had steamed, the room filling with the fog of their desire.

She wanted him again. She wanted to lose herself this way, in lovemaking, instead of how she'd lost herself before. In alcohol and drugs and back alleys. If only she'd known Ty sooner…

But she had. A lifetime ago. She hadn't been with the Bowerses long when they'd brought her to the hospital that night, when Richard had been having chest pains. Maybe that was how they'd easily forgotten her in the waiting room. And she'd found Ty instead, the boy five or six years older than her but every bit as lost and alone.

Unconscious even. But yet he remembered her. He could read her the way she read him. He'd proved it tonight, when he'd made love to her, bringing her a pleasure she was certain she'd never known…even though there was so much she'd forgotten.

Like where she'd lived. She'd been going to school—she remembered that. Maybe she'd lived on campus. No, she was too old for a dormitory. Thoughts skipped through her head, jumbled memories just beyond her comprehension. But then the light evaporated, darkness rolling into the room despite the lamp burning beside the bed.

Although she was pressed tight against him, she couldn't see Ty. Not a glimpse of his muscled chest. Not a strand of his black hair. Not a glint of his blue eyes.

All she saw was black. Then the sparks glittered. Bits of red. Fire this time, instead of blood. She heard the crackle of it. Inside her head?

Justice. Ty McIntyre wasn't a witch, but because of his interference he deserved to die like one.

Burned alive. With the witch who'd orchestrated his downfall.

Her head pounded with Donovan Roarke's pain, with his madness. Her blood hummed with the hatred flowing through his veins, gripping his body.

Gasoline burned his hands as it ran over his skin. He tossed it onto the fire, spurring the flames higher. Making it burn brighter and faster. Soon. Soon Ty McIntyre would be dead. And the witch would die with him. Then, when the embers cooled, he could pick through their ashes for the little crescent moon, for the charm that was his.

Smoke drifted under the bedroom door, burning Irina's nose and eyes. She blinked and coughed, then thumped her fist against Ty's chest. "Wake up. Ty, wake up!"

He barely shifted on the mattress. Had the smoke already overcome him? She threw back the covers and reached for her clothes. She'd get them out of the house before the fire consumed it and them, before Roarke succeeded.

But for the charm. He wouldn't find it in their ashes. It wasn't here. She remembered now where she'd been living when she'd heard her mother's scream. She knew where the charm would be—if she hadn't sold it. She had to live to get the little sliver of moon.

"Come on," Ty said, pulling the sweater over her head as he had the scrubs at the hospital, as if she were a helpless child.

He'd already dressed, while she fumbled with her jeans. Wide-awake as if he'd never slept as soundly as she'd watched him sleep. He was alert and ready for anything.

The death Donovan Roarke had planned for him?

She sucked in a breath, more fearful for his safety than hers. "If we run out of here…"

"He'll shoot us," Ty finished for her. He couldn't read minds—except maybe hers—but somehow he knew that Roarke had set the fire, that Roarke waited outside to prevent their escape.

Even though he'd never been inside the madman's head, he knew him as well as Irina did, maybe better. Despite the heat, goose bumps rose along her skin. Fear ran cold through her veins. "What are we going to do?"

If they didn't bust out of the house, they would burn alive just as the maniac intended. Just as he'd killed her mother. Glass crackled, breaking either from the heat or from a bullet.

"I can't believe the son of a bitch found us," Ty murmured as he headed into the bathroom. The pipes groaned as he ran water. He came back with dripping towels. "Hold this over your head."

As a plan, it wasn't much—not like Roarke's. Either Ty had shut her out again or he had no idea how they could escape with their lives. He closed his hand over hers. "Irina, do you trust me?"

She nodded. She hadn't at first, not when he'd first entered her head or her hospital room, but now that she really knew who he was, he was the only person she trusted. Uncertain if he'd seen her affirmative gesture under the towel, she said, "Yes."

"Then follow me."

When he opened the bedroom door, smoke funneled into the room. The hall wasn't engulfed yet, but just a few yards away the living room and kitchen were ablaze. Two doors down the hall, closer to the flames, he opened another door to a staircase. Closing his hand around her wrist, he dragged her down the steps, feeling his way in the dark. While the smoke was thinner here, above them the house groaned and shuddered as the fire consumed it. Flames crackled and boards creaked, beginning to splinter.

"It's going to cave in on us," she said, her voice cracking from the smoke and the fear that gripped her. Maybe she'd been wrong to trust him, to trust her own judgment considering how she'd been living a short time ago.

Would she be living at all much longer?

"This is our only chance," Ty told her, then beseeched her as he had at the hospital. "Trust me."

He'd saved her at the hospital, but he'd no more than uttered his appeal when a joist broke above their heads, the crack rising sharply above the roar of the flames. Burning boards collapsed into the basement, the fire springing up in a ring around them.

Startled, Irina jerked from his grasp and stumbled back. Her mother's thoughts, in her last terrified moments, rolled back through Irina's mind. Her screams. Her pain. Irina threw up her arms, fending off the horrific memories as much as the flames. Then she tripped, sprawling across the cold dirt floor of the old Michigan basement. Her neck arched, she just missed striking her head on the unforgiving surface.

Maybe it would have been better if she'd struck her head, if she were passed out and the smoke took her before the flames. She didn't want to burn alive the way her mother had. Fear paralyzed her, and she lay frozen on the basement floor.

"Irina!" Ty called out, his voice a harsh rasp of fear. For her.

Before he could reach for her, another joist broke and a wall dropped into the basement, the wallpaper on it melting and turning black as it dissolved into the broken drywall. The burning barrier separated them from each other. Her on one side of the wall, him on the other.

Then more of the floor gave way, another joist dropping in on them, falling across her legs, pinning Irina to the floor so that even if she'd had the courage to move, she couldn't. Just like when she'd been restrained to the bed in the psychiatric ward, she was trapped and helpless.

Waiting for death.

Chapter 7

Heedless of the heat, Ty knocked his fist through the wall of fire, reaching for her. He wasn't going to lose her now, not when it had taken him so long to find her.

"Irina, grab my hand," he commanded her, ignoring the pain as the flames lapped at his skin.

She shook her head, her hair tangling in the dirt of the basement floor and the hot ash falling from above. Her eyes wide with fear, she murmured, "No…"

Determined to save her, he kicked aside the burning debris, knocking down the wall that separated them. The studs and drywall collapsed into broken splinters and ash. Then he leaned down and he hefted off the joist that had fallen across her legs.

"I've got you," he said as she vaulted to her feet and into his arms. Smoke clung to her hair, soot streaking her face. "You're okay."

"We're still trapped, Ty," she said, holding tight to his back, her fingers clenched in his shirt.

"No, we're not." He dropped a kiss on her lips, tasting smoke. "Remember, I said I'd protect you."

She nodded, but he could see the struggle going on inside her, the struggle to trust him. The struggle not to fall apart. Again.

"I trust you," she repeated, but he couldn't help wondering who she was trying to convince, him or herself.

His hands on her shoulders, he pushed her back. "I'm going to get us out of here," he assured her.

Her head bobbed in a nervous nod as she clutched at him, obviously scared to lose contact with him again.

He caught her wrist, pulling her hand from his shirt. Ignoring the burn from where the flames had brushed his skin, he wrapped his fingers around her thin wrist, then dragged her behind him. They scrambled across smoldering boards and crushed boxes toward the cement stairs that led up to a set of metal doors. She'd kept up with him, her fingers gripping his forearm. Strength and determination glowed in her dark eyes.

He released her to grab the inside handles and rattle the doors in their frames. They were locked. From the outside.

"Goddamn him," Irina yelled, blinking back tears of frustration as she slammed her fists against the metal doors. "He made sure we couldn't get out."

Ty shook his head. Roarke wasn't the monster who'd put the chain through the outside handles, securing it with a padlock to keep Ty inside, imprisoned in the basement so he couldn't get out, so he couldn't tell anyone what his father had done to him.

Her hand, the knuckles scraped from the metal, closed around his arm. "I'm sorry…."

He was a sorry son of a bitch, but Ty wasn't going to let the heartless bastard hurt him anymore. He pushed against the doors, rattling the metal.

"Roarke could be up there, waiting," she cautioned, her voice quavering with fear. The flames from the other side of the basement cast light and chased shadows around her face. Her dark eyes reflected back the fire.

He shoved against the doors again. They gave

some more. The chain was old and had to be rusted. If he kept fighting, he could break the links. He could get them free.

"We're going to have to take that chance." Ty would rather take a bullet than be burned alive.

Ty hoped Donovan Roarke was waiting for them because he was going to kill the psychopath with his bare hands. Anger coursed through him, giving him the strength to force up the rusted, locked doors. Links snapped on the chain, but still the doors wouldn't give, the hinges rusted and unable to budge. Again and again he rammed his shoulder against the metal. The hinges snapped and the doors finally wedged open, not far but enough for them to escape.

He squeezed through the opening, the branches of overgrown shrubs grabbing at his clothes and scratching his face and arms. He gasped for fresh air. But here, this close to the blazing house, he sucked in only a lungful of smoke. The smoke burned his eyes, blinding him. If Roarke stood beside him, he couldn't see him.

Ty had to take the chance that the madman hadn't found this exit, concealed by unkempt landscaping, weeds woven into the overgrown shrubs. He reached back into the doors and pulled Irina out through the opening. The house shuddered as the flames ate it from the inside out. He jerked Irina's arm, dragging her back across the yard just as the house imploded, collapsing into the basement in a shower of sparks and rising flames that lapped at them, the heat burning.

Ty scrambled to his feet and lifted Irina up. She coughed and sputtered as he pulled her behind him, running through the backyard into the alley. Hopefully the smoke would conceal their flight, and Roarke wouldn't know that he'd failed, that they lived.

Keeping Irina close to his side, Ty ducked into the shadow of the garages that lined the alley. Back pressed to the old wood siding, he moved from building to building, testing the lock on each one. Knobs refused to turn. He'd pick the locks if he had to, but he'd rather not spend any more time in the open, where Roarke might see them. Finally one knob turned and a service door opened. He slipped inside, pulling Irina behind him. Then he turned and locked the door behind them.

Irina dropped to her knees on the cement, her breathing coming in ragged gasps. Her shoulders shook.

"Are you all right?" he asked, running his fingers through her smoke- and soot-encrusted hair.

She glanced up at him and nodded. In the faint

light coming through the windows in the garage door, he caught the glimmer of tears in her eyes, streaming down her cheeks.

His eyes burned from the smoke, scratchy and dry. Like his throat. God, it had been close. Too damned close.

"You saved me," she said. "Again."

"I told you I'd protect you." *Or die trying.*

"It's that last part I worry about," she said, speaking to his thought. "I don't want you getting hurt because of me."

He'd only get hurt if she did. That realization frightened him more than the fire had; she meant too much to him, more than anyone ever had. "Irina…"

"I know."

Of course she did. She knew his every thought, his every feeling…probably better than he did. While he'd once resented her invasion of his mind, he'd resigned himself to it now. He couldn't fight her, not now. He had to concentrate all his energy on fighting Roarke.

Ty ran his shaking hand through his hair. Even in the dimly lit garage, he could see his fingers came away black. How had Roarke found him so quickly? Was the son of a bitch psychic? Had killing Irina's mother, a witch, given him some supernatural power, the way Eli's journal had claimed?

No, Ty refused to believe there was anything special about Roarke. He was just a good investigator. Just because Ty hadn't told anyone about his properties didn't mean Roarke couldn't search deeds and find out. He expelled a ragged breath. He and Irina might be out of the fire, but they were still trapped, his truck and cell phone having gone up in the flames.

Then he leaned back, and metal shifted beneath his spine. He turned to the car behind him. An old Mustang. He might be able to hot-wire it, but he hoped he wouldn't have to and reached in the wheel well. Sure enough, his fingers closed over the magnetic hide-away key container.

"You found the key. We can get out of here now," Irina said, expelling a ragged sigh of relief.

In the dim light he noted the expression she wore, that one where she looked as if her eyes couldn't see, only her ears could hear. "Irina, are you okay?"

She nodded. "He thinks we're in the fire. He doesn't know yet that we escaped. We have to get out of here before he realizes…"

"That he failed again?" Satisfaction eased some of the anger eating at Ty over the madman's latest attempt.

"When he realizes…" She blinked, and her dark eyes, wide with fear, focused.

"He'll be even more dangerous."

"More determined to kill *you*," she said, her voice trembling, "as well as my sisters and me."

The witches.

"I'm taking you to your sisters. David's beefed up the security at the penthouse so it's like Fort Knox. Roarke can't get to you there," he promised as he helped her up from the floor. Maybe he should have taken her to the penthouse that first night, before he'd gotten so close to her, before he'd made love to her.

His stomach lurched as he realized what his friend might be thinking. "Damn, if they see the news and think we were in the house…"

"Why would they think that?"

"My name's on the deed. That's how Roarke found us. Even then, David knows the house. He grew up just down the street from here." But in an entirely different environment with parents who had always loved him, even when they'd struggled to understand him. "Your sisters must be going through hell. I have to bring you to them. Now."

"No," she said, every bit as insistent as she'd been from the beginning. "We'll find a phone. We'll call them and let them know that we're fine."

Frustration frayed his patience, so he snapped at her, "Why are you stalling? You know they don't give a damn whether or not you have the charm. They want to *see* you, to make sure you're safe. They love you."

And he was afraid that if they stayed alone together much longer, so would he.

A smile lifted her full lips, and her dark eyes gleamed brightly in the faint light. God, she'd heard him again and knew how close he was to falling…

"I know where the charm is," she said, pulling open the driver's door of the Mustang.

She wasn't about to tell him where the charm was so he could retrieve it on his own. He didn't have to read her stubborn mind to know that. He shook his head, unable to fight the grin tugging at his mouth. "Damn you, woman."

"I feel the same way," she said, reaching up to press a kiss against his lips before she scooted across the seat to the passenger side.

At least she was going to let him drive. Still shaking his head, he rolled up the old wooden garage door. Outside, smoke hung heavy like fog, thick and impenetrable. He had to trust her gift, had to believe that Roarke still didn't know yet that they had escaped. Trust had never come easy for Ty.

"We have to hurry," she said, her voice a breathy, urgent whisper.

He folded his body into the old leather seat,

then jammed the key in the ignition. The engine turned but didn't catch. He pumped the gas pedal and tried again. The engine rolled over with a sickening metallic clank of gears, then it finally caught. The car vibrated as the engine, unused for so long, fought to stay running.

"This thing might not get us far," he warned her.

"We don't have far to go," she said.

Did she refer to the distance to where she'd left the charm or to the entire witch hunt? God, he hoped it was almost over, that they'd finally be able to stop Roarke before he killed again.

Ty left off the lights as he drove down the back alley, the car bouncing over ruts in the crumbled asphalt. Around the garages and through the backyards he glimpsed the burning rubble of his old house.

She slid her hand over his thigh, squeezing. "I'm sorry, Ty."

"No. It's something I should have done a long time ago." Now the memories weren't only buried, they were burned to sparking embers. Maybe he'd finally be able to let his past go, all of it.

Even her?

"You're sure this is the place?" Ty asked. "You don't have a key hidden around here?"

"Where could I hide a key?" she asked, as she leaned against the railing behind him, watching as he picked the lock of the apartment door. Faint doubt filtered through her. Was this the right number? She had so many missing or blurred sections of her life, thanks to alcohol, drugs and all the damned voices in her head.

She fisted her hands against the wood, stilling their trembling. She could have used the Vicodin now, to settle her nerves, but the little pills had gone up in the fire, the way *they* almost had.

She drew in a deep breath. She didn't need drugs or alcohol; she didn't want to numb herself and black out. She wanted to remember. She *had* to.

Other numbers, doors and places drifted through her mind. Dorm rooms. Campus apartments. This was an off-campus development, a ten-unit apartment building perched on the edge of a deep ravine. Beyond the outside second-story walkway on which they stood, trees swayed in a brisk night breeze. Even with the fresh air, all she smelled was the acrid smoke from the house fire embedded deep in her hair and skin, burned in her nostrils.

She wrinkled her nose, longing for a hot shower, a soft bed…and all those missing pieces of her memory. "I'm sorry I don't have the key," she said as Ty continued to slide his tools into the lock.

"Me, too," he muttered around the metal rod he clenched between his teeth while he used other ones to work the tumblers of the deadbolt.

"You don't think anyone's in there?" she asked, nerves fluttering through her stomach. Her memories were so jumbled, how could she trust any of them?

"We knocked," Ty reminded her.

And no one had answered. Yet how could she have afforded such an apartment on her own? "I must have had a roommate...."

Ty turned, glancing over his broad shoulder at her. Soot streaked his face. With a lift of that scarred eyebrow, he asked a question. *A man?*

She'd never really dated a man. She knew that now, after being with him. She'd only dated boys.

If they found the charm inside, he'd drop the little crescent moon and her off to her sisters. Would he walk away then, his job done?

He didn't want to care about her. About anyone. He didn't want to need anyone. She drew in a shaky breath. He was strong, far stronger than she'd ever been. With his will and determination, she didn't have to read his mind to know what he would do. He would walk away.

She didn't need the drugs and alcohol anymore, but she feared she needed him. Too much.

The lock clicked and the doorknob turned beneath Ty's hand. She jerked away from the railing to stand close behind him, her hands clenching the sooty cotton of his T-shirt. "You did it!"

"Let me go in alone," he said.

Not the way he had at his house, to deal with old memories under the guise of securing the premises. Her heart lurched as images from the Bowerses' house flitted through her mind. The tattered yellow police tape and the blood spray on the wall. He didn't want her walking into another crime scene or finding a body.

She understood that and appreciated his concern. But even though she wasn't as strong as he was, she wasn't as weak as she'd been. She'd come out from behind the Dumpster. She'd outrun a killer. So far.

She was far stronger than she'd realized. Pretty soon he wouldn't be around to protect her, to save her. She had to learn to take care of herself. "I can handle it, Ty. I can handle whatever we find."

He didn't argue with her, either aloud or in his head. Did he believe what she still struggled to accept—her strength?

"It's not like we're even sure this is where I lived," she pointed out.

"I thought you were sure." Or he'd just broken into someone else's apartment. He could add breaking and entering to the other crimes he'd committed.

Her heart softened, and she laid her cheek against his shoulder blade. He'd done so much for her, given up so much. He had a greater chance of going to jail than returning to his job. And maybe because of her, because she didn't want to meet her sisters yet, he might have lost the friends he had, the few people he'd let close to him.

But not as close as she was. Words burned in her dry throat, words she wanted to tell him. But her feelings would only frighten him away; he wasn't ready to hear how she felt. He wouldn't believe her.

"I'm sure," she said—of her feelings. Of the apartment, she couldn't trust her memory.

"Okay," he said, pushing open the door and reaching for the light switch.

On the tables flanking the couch, lamps flickered on, the dim bulbs casting eerie shadows around the chocolate-painted living room. Not that the place looked much like a living room with the dried herbs hanging from hooks in the ceiling and the candles and crystals on every flat surface.

His breath shuddered out. "Apparently we have the right place." *And Roarke was right. She is a witch.*

Irina gazed around at the hanging herbs. At the crystals sparkling like diamonds in the dim lamplight.

Had she practiced witchcraft?

Donovan stood across the street from the burning house, mingling with the neighbors and other gawkers who watched the blaze. Firefighters sprayed water on the inferno, but there was no stopping the flames. Despite what the orange spires had devoured, they were still hungry for more.

Like him.

He'd killed another witch.

He closed his eyes on a wave of dizziness. Where was the infusion of power he'd felt with the deaths of the others? With *her mother's* death?

When he opened his eyes, *she* wavered before him in the smoke, glowing orange, her dark eyes molten, her hair flames. The ghost of Myra Cooper, the mother to the three witches. He'd killed her what seemed so long ago now, but she continued to haunt him.

She wouldn't give him peace until they were all

dead. He was certain of it. He wouldn't be strong enough to banish her to hell until he got the charms.

How long before he could dig through the ashes of the house and find the little pewter crescent moon? How long before the flames would not be able to spring back to life and overtake him the way he imagined in his dream?

It was only a dream, a nightmare of the witches circling him, laughing as they burned him alive. It wasn't a vision; he'd gotten some of the powers of the dead witch—her ability to see ghosts and the future—but that wasn't *his* future.

It had been *hers*. Irina Cooper's.

Where was her ghost? Why wasn't *she* with her mother, dancing in the fire?

Of all those he'd killed, only Myra Cooper haunted him, she being the only true witch. But Irina Cooper, with her witchcraft, her ability to read his mind, she was most definitely a witch, too.

Where was she?

Along with the pain pounding in his head, anxiety gripped his heart, clenching it in a tight fist. He pushed through the crowd, people murmuring protests as he shoved them aside and crossed the street.

A police barricade and the line of fire trucks

blocked his access to the burning pyre. "Sir," a female officer said, "you need to step back. Clear the street."

"I…uh…" he stammered, the smoke burning his eyes, his nose. He shouldn't be standing so close to the cop. If she smelled the gasoline on his hands, his clothes…

But he had to know. "The man who lives here—"

"We were told no one lives here," the officer interrupted, tensing with obvious alarm. "The neighbors assured us the house was vacant. The last tenants had moved out a few months ago." She studied him through narrowed eyes.

He knew the look. The furrow of her brow as she concentrated on what he'd said and what he hadn't. The flare of suspicion in her eyes. He should back away before she reached for her gun, before she signaled the other officers on the scene.

But he had to know.

"A friend of mine—the landlord—was staying here," he continued. "A woman was staying with him."

She reached for the transmitter at the collar of her shirt and pressed the button. "Tell the firefighters to check the house for two bodies. A man and a woman." She leaned over and lifted the police tape. "Sir, why don't you join me over here? I have a few questions for you."

He couldn't afford to get any closer, couldn't afford to answer any questions. Yet he ducked under the tape, getting closer to the fire where Myra Cooper's ghost danced. Was she taunting him?

The officer's radio crackled. "They're searching, sir," she relayed to him. "Tell me the names of the people you believe might be in the house."

House? There was nothing left now but the debris burning in the hole in the ground.

"I don't know the woman." At least not what name she answered to. Was it the name her adoptive parents had given her—Heather Bowers? Or was it real name, her real identity—Irina Cooper?

"And the man?"

"Ty McIntyre."

She gasped. "He's wanted for questioning."

Roarke wanted him, too. Dead. With the witch. But more than that, he wanted the charm.

The radio chattered again. He caught the gist of the message given to her: no bodies had been found inside. He had to ask, "What if there was nothing left to find?"

But ashes.

She shook her head. "The fire was hot, so that could have been an issue. But they found cellar doors in the back. Someone forced them open from inside the basement. We believe Ty McIntyre escaped."

Son of a bitch! And because he was so honorable, he wouldn't have left without saving the witch. And the charm.

Roarke turned toward the last dying flames of the fire and the woman who hovered above them. Her mouth was open, not in the scream she'd uttered in her last moments before the fire had consumed her.

No, her mouth was open in laughter, taunting him.

Chapter 8

"This stuff can't be mine," Irina insisted as she ran her fingers over the smooth crystals laid across her chocolate-stained mission coffee table. The stones were cool to her touch. The scent of lavender and sandalwood wafted down from the herbs hanging over her head. "I would have remembered…."

"If you were a witch?"

"I am a witch, Ty," she admitted what she'd fought remembering for so long, what she'd struggled to believe. "That's what Donovan Roarke believes. That's why he wants to kill me. That and the tumor in his brain."

"We found out about that by hacking into his doctor's computer and reading his medical records," Ty said. "How do you know about that?"

She reminded him, "I've been in his head."

"That can't be a fun place." Despite his flip remark, his blue eyes softened with sympathy, and he lifted his arms as if to hold her. But then he walked away.

"It's a horrible, demented place." She sighed, her breath escaping in a ragged gasp. "I spend more time in other people's heads than my own. Maybe that's why there's so much I can't remember. This life."

"What *do* you remember?" he asked as he moved around the spacious apartment, peering through the open doorways off the short hall.

She followed him, glancing into each of the two bedrooms. The closet doors of the first one, painted a dark bloodred, stood open, the rod empty of clothes, hangers scattered about the tan carpeting. Someone had left in a hurry. Had it been her?

The closet of the other bedroom, painted a deep cinnamon, was filled, so many colorful clothes jammed in that the doors wouldn't close. Toiletries spilled across the dresser top. Makeup. Hers? She walked over to the dresser and picked up a lipstick in a brilliant burgundy. Her color?

She could scarcely remember her things, let alone her life.

She noticed an oak jewelry box, the mirrored lid hanging open, the velvet compartments cleaned out. Had she taken everything and pawned or traded it for alcohol, for drugs? If the charm had been inside, she would have done the same with it. She hoped this wasn't her room, her apartment.

She followed Ty back into the living room.

"I remember going to school," she answered him finally. "I also worked at the school."

"As what?" he asked as he walked into the kitchen, opening and closing all of the white cupboard doors. A few boxes and cans sat on the shelves, but no charm glinted in the pendant lights hanging from the ceiling.

Irina peered into the pantry, where a trash can overflowed with empty liquor bottles. God, she probably had lived here.

He walked back into the living room, his limp more pronounced. Had he reinjured his leg in the fire?

She shut the pantry door and followed him back to where the dried herbs hung low over the couch, in front of the fireplace. Built-in shelves, the same white as the mantel, flanked the fireplace.

"I was a student advisor," she remembered. "I even had a group."

"A coven?"

She smacked his shoulder. "No. I had a support group for adopted children." She picked up a picture from the sofa table behind the brown leather couch, a picture of her and another dark-haired woman. She hadn't been wrong about the apartment number; this was her place. "I met *her* there."

Ty only glanced at the picture yet probably took in every detail. "She looks like you."

"I look like a lot of people or you wouldn't have gotten me out of the hospital." She studied him as he moved around the living room, checking out every herb, every candle. "Do you regret that?"

"What?" He turned toward her. The scarred eyebrow lifted with his question.

She hadn't been able to read his thoughts or his emotions since they'd stepped inside her apartment. Was he repulsed? Disillusioned?

"Do you wish you would have left me in there?" she asked him.

"Irina," he said, his dark blue eyes widening with shock. "You know Roarke would have gotten you—"

"If you hadn't." She sighed as regret poured

through her, not over what they'd done but what she'd cost him. "But you'd have your house—"

"I hated that house," he said, a muscle twitching in his rigidly held jaw. "I should have burned it down myself. Roarke just beat me to it."

"But your truck, your stuff—you even lost your cell phone."

"I can get another cell phone." He hadn't, though. He'd stopped at a pay phone to call David and assure his friend that they were all right, no matter what the television news reported.

"You lost your job, too. You won't get it back now…because of me." He might even have lost his freedom over her.

He sighed now and dragged a soot-covered hand through his hair. "Damn it, Irina. You can hear my thoughts. Why are you going to make me say it?"

"Because I *need* to hear you say it." She needed reassurance. Although she knew he didn't think he was good at giving comfort, she needed it only from him.

"You mean more to me than any of that stuff, than any of this!" He gestured around the apartment, at the herbs and crystals. "I don't care what you do. I know *who* you are."

She gazed around again. This might have been

her apartment, but she didn't remember having all the witchcraft stuff. Tarot cards covered the coffee table, the faces obscured by the crystals. "That makes one of us."

"Irina, stop beating yourself up. And help me look for the charm."

He was right. She lifted her chin, summoning her pride and the strength she'd only found a few days ago in an alley because he'd told her to stop hiding. She was good at hiding. If she'd hidden something in the apartment, where would she have put it?

Behind something, the way she'd cowered behind the Dumpster. She searched around the knickknacks, amazed at the odd assortment arranged haphazardly on the shelves. A snow globe of a cornfield fascinated her. When she shook the globe, crows rained down onto the stalks and the scarecrow standing guard in the middle. A shiver raced up and down her spine.

"What's that?" Ty asked.

She shrugged. "I don't know. It's weird." She extended her arm to set it back on the bookshelf, but the lamplight glinted off something metal at the back of the shelf. She put the globe aside to reach for the shiny bit.

As her fingertips moved over it, the metal

warmed her skin. She picked it up and laid it in her palm, then stared down at the sliver of pewter moon. She hadn't pawned it or lost it. She'd had it all this time, hidden away.

"Ty, I found it."

He was already next to her. His hands closed over her shoulders, squeezing. "That's it." His breath blew across her cheek as he leaned over to peer closer at the charm. "We have it."

"Do you really think it has magical powers?" The warmth radiating from the moon suggested it did, but she didn't know. She'd had it all this time and she couldn't remember it ever doing anything for her. But then, she was still alive, so maybe it had done what it was supposed to.

Now she had to do what she was supposed to— reunite with her sisters.

"Ariel and Elena believe it has some special power," Ty reminded her. "So does Roarke."

"He thinks the charms will save him from the tumor," she said. "That's why he wants all of them."

"For power," Ty said. He reached out and ran a fingertip over the charm. "It's warm."

"It feels alive."

"It's supposed to keep whoever has it alive."

She stared at the little bit of ancient metal. "I have all this stuff in my apartment." But she was pretty certain she'd never used it. "I hear people's thoughts—"

"Telepathy."

"But I don't know if I can believe in this." She closed her fingers over the charm, embedding it in her palm as she made a fist. No power infused her; she didn't feel stronger.

Not strong enough to meet her sisters, to face the disappointment they must surely feel in her. They knew where she'd been living, how she'd barely been living, where she'd wound up…what a mess she'd been. She wasn't strong, not the way they'd been throughout the witch hunt. They'd never run. They'd never hidden.

"Maybe it's enough that your sisters believe," Ty said. "I'll bring you to them now. You have no excuse."

But fear built in her—not fear of Roarke or death, fear of disappointing more people who wanted to love her, like the Bowerses. They'd wound up dying over her. She didn't want the same fate to befall her sisters. They believed the charms, reunited with the sisters, would end the witch hunt. She wasn't sure what she believed in anymore.

"I reek of smoke," she said, grappling for more time. "I want to take a shower first."

He couldn't argue with that. He wouldn't mind one himself.

"Join me, then," she invited him.

"Irina…"

She reached up, twining her arms around his neck to pull his head down for her kiss. His mouth consumed hers, his tongue pushing through her lips to tease and torment hers. Stroking, as his body had stroked hers, so passionately.

"Ty…" she moaned.

"Shower," he groaned against her lips, backing her toward the hall.

She reached for the door of the bathroom, remembering the tan tile floor and shower, the walls glowing with a warm orange glaze. She flipped on the light and tugged Ty inside with her, closing them into the small, romantic room. So unlike the stark bathroom where they'd made love just before Roarke had set the fire.

She shook her head, refusing to think about anything but Ty and making love with him. She turned toward the sink, where candles stood, but as she reached for the matches beside them, she pulled back as if they were already lit and ready to burn her.

"No fire," Ty agreed.

Her breath shuddered out. "No."

"Just water," he said as he turned on the faucet in the shower. Then he reached for her sweater, lifting up the hem. "And skin."

"Just skin," she agreed as she tugged up his T-shirt. Dropping them onto the tile floor, they shed their sooty clothes, then stood naked before each other.

Irina's nipples hardened under Ty's passionate gaze. When he reached out, she knocked his hand away. His eyebrow, with that jagged little scar running through it, lifted. "What?"

"We're filthy."

"Not yet," he teased, "but I intend to do some things to you—"

"We're covered in soot."

"I don't care," he said as he dragged her up against him. His hand cupped the back of her head as he devoured her mouth, his lips sipping at hers, his tongue sliding in and out with delicious friction.

She shivered despite the heat of his passion. His mouth smiled against hers, only half tipping up in that little lopsided grin she loved so much. He bore so many scars from his childhood, both physical and emotional. Would he ever let himself feel for her as she did him?

But maybe she shouldn't trust her feelings.

Maybe in a little while she wouldn't remember him any better than she remembered other parts of her life. Her heart lurched at the thought of forgetting him.

Never.

She would make such memories with him that they couldn't be forgotten, they'd forever be branded into her mind, her heart, her soul. "Ty, make love to me."

"You're dirty," he reminded her as he opened the shower door and stepped inside under the hot spray. Then he caught her wrist, and as he'd pulled her from burning debris back at his house, he pulled her inside with him.

She closed the door with trembling fingers, enclosing them into the warm blanket of heat, the dreamy mist of steam and the caress of the pulsating water. Black rivulets of soot ran from Ty's dark hair, over his face, down the muscular contours of his chest and lower. Irina reached for the soap to wash him, but his hand closed over hers, and he took away the slippery bar.

Then he soaped his hands, using them as a washcloth, running them along her throat and shoulders, down over her breasts. His palms stroked over her nipples until her head fell back and she uttered a moan.

Then his hands were in her hair, working a liberal glob of shampoo through the soot-tangled curls. "You're so beautiful," he murmured.

If anyone had ever told her that before, she didn't remember. Her heart swelled, and a giddy rush filled her, making her dizzy with passion. "Ty…"

He shifted her so she stood under the spray, the water washing the shampoo from her hair, sending suds over her naked skin, cleansing away the soot and smoke…and every trace of the life she'd once lived in despair. Staring into his dark blue eyes, she felt hope burgeon. She felt anything was possible for her now. A normal life. A love.

"Ty." She reached for him, winding her arms around his neck, sliding her wet, soapy body against his, skin against skin.

He groaned and shifted away, dropping to his knees. He lifted her so that her legs straddled his shoulders. She floundered for handholds, grabbing at the top of the shower door and the built-in soap dish. He held her with one hand on her back while his other reached up and encircled her breast, his thumb flicking over her wet nipple.

Irina's breath caught, burning in her lungs as her heart pounded against her ribs.

He licked the inside of each of her thighs,

turning his head from side to side, sipping water off her skin as it ran down her body. The stubble of his beard scraped against her thighs, a delicious contrast to the slick caress of his mouth and tongue. Then his mouth moved, his tongue stroking through her wet curls. His hand shifted on her breast and he plucked at the nipple, teasing it.

Her passion for him raged, burning in her stomach and lower. He slid his tongue inside her, slick and wet against the most sensitive part of her.

Irina's head fell back against the tile wall. And she weakly protested, "Ty, no…"

But he was relentless, sliding his tongue in and out, lapping at her, until she shattered in his arms. Orgasms crashed through her, breaking her apart, until she melted against the tile wall, spent.

But not done. She wanted more than he'd given her. She wanted to give. She rose up on shaking legs, pulling him up with her. Then she kissed him, tasting her own passion on his lips. His tongue slid into her mouth, making love to it the way he had her body.

She reached for the soap, lathering up her hands before she reached for him. His penis was hard and long. She remembered how it had stretched her, how she hadn't thought she could take in all that

he was. But she had. He'd filled her completely.
She moved her hand up and down the wet, slippery
length of him, stroking.

He closed his eyes and groaned her name,
"Irina…"

*She was asking too much of him. Control.
Something he wasn't sure he could hold on to if
she kept touching him.*

His thought didn't frighten her. She wasn't
worried about his losing control. She wanted him
to. She dropped to her knees, then replaced her
hand with her mouth, sliding it up and down the
length of him. Taking him as deep as she could.

His hands fisted in her hair. "Irina…"

Then he came, spilling his passion into her
mouth until it dripped from her chin. The shower
spray washed it off, washed them clean.

But it wasn't enough. He wasn't satisfied. His
blue eyes ablaze with desire, he lifted her, his
biceps straining. Her legs encircled his waist and
he drove his penis, still throbbing with orgasm,
into her. Their skin slick with water and passion,
their bodies slapped. His hands cupped her
buttocks, squeezing and lifting so she rode him.

Then he reached between them, flicking his
finger over her most sensitive part until she shattered again. Heat and pleasure tore through her

while her love for him completed her in a way she had never been.

She loved him. But knowing how he felt about love, she doubted she'd ever tell him.

Too bad he couldn't read her mind.

Ty propped himself on his elbow, watching how her lashes shadowed her cheek as she slept. How her breasts rose and fell with each deep breath, lifting the chocolate-colored satin sheets and comforter. He should awaken her, bring her to Ariel and Elena. They had the charm, and he had no excuse to keep her to himself any longer.

Could she hear his thoughts now, when she slept? She'd been in his head so long. Now she was in his heart. Did she know how he felt about her?

And that he didn't want to feel that way about anyone? They had no future. He didn't want to marry. He wanted no family. He couldn't risk becoming the monster his father had been. The cycle of abuse haunted him like those buried and now burned memories. He couldn't risk it, not even for her. *Especially* not with her.

She jolted awake, her body jerking as her eyes flew open. "Ty!"

"I'm here, I'm here," he assured her, pulling her tight in his arms.

She shuddered against him. "You're awake."

He hadn't forgiven himself for falling asleep earlier, when Roarke set the house on fire. When he'd called David last night, his friend had blasted him for not answering his cell. He'd been calling to warn them about a vision Elena had had, a vision of him and Irina dying in a fire. Even though he hadn't answered the phone, he should have been more vigilant.

If Irina hadn't woke him up…

"Shh…" she said, nuzzling into his neck. "Go back to sleep."

"I can't sleep," he said, and not just because morning light streamed through the white wooden blinds and lit up her bedroom. "He might have found your name on the lease."

"It isn't. It's Maria's apartment."

"The girl from the picture."

"She invited me to live with her. She's the one with money." Her breath caught, and she stared up at him with wide eyes. "Where do you think she is?"

"I don't know. If this is your room," he said, glancing around the cluttered space, "then she cleaned hers out. She must have moved out."

"In a hurry," Irina said, her voice soft with fear for her friend. "Do you think Roarke found her and did what he did to the Bowerses…?"

"Your name isn't on the lease," he reminded her. Not that Roarke couldn't have found her friend another way. As he'd proven again and again, the man was a damned good investigator. But then, so was Ty.

"I can look for her," he offered, "after I bring you to your sisters."

"Where are *they?*"

"I'd say they're both at David's penthouse." Waiting for him, wondering where the hell he was. He didn't have to read David's mind to know his friend was furious.

"Fort Knox."

He couldn't remember what he'd told her, or what she knew. "David's engaged to Ariel."

"He's your best friend."

Was. He wasn't sure David would ever speak to him again after this. Ty had had her for two days and not brought her to see them. He was certain they were all at the penthouse, waiting for him to finally bring Irina to them. Ariel and Elena were probably every bit as angry as David.

"I'm sorry," she murmured, "that I've been so stubborn."

"You were right," he conceded. If they were truly his friends, they'd find a way to forgive him. If not…he'd never minded being alone. But that had been before he'd met Irina, before he'd held her in his arms…in his heart.

He glanced down, afraid that she might have read his mind. But she had that unfocused look on her face, her eyes staring blindly at the ceiling.

"It was the right thing to find the charm first," he said, hoping his friends would understand that. Now when they reunited, all three sisters would be safe.

And Roarke would be in trouble. He'd try for them when they were all together, and between Ty and David's security team, they wouldn't let the psychopath slip away again.

She brushed her hair back from her face, her hand shaking slightly. "I don't want to meet up with my sisters at a penthouse."

Frustration tightened the muscles in his stomach. "Irina, you're stalling."

Again. The way she had in the shower. Using him.

"I'm not—"

"They love you," he said, anger surging through him. "They've been longing to see you. They don't care where you've been—"

"On the streets," she said, her voice thick with self-loathing.

"Homeless."

"I had a home. With the Bowerses." Her breath

caught, and her eyes glistened with unshed tears. "Here. I had a life, a future…."

"Until Roarke started up the witch hunt again. It's *his* fault," he argued, "not yours. He's to blame for everything bad that's happened."

She nodded. "Yes. It all started when he killed my mother. That's when my world fell apart."

Understanding, with dread, washed over him. "You heard her murder."

She nodded again, her teeth sinking into her bottom lip as she fought back the tears again. "That's when I left here—or class. I don't remember where I was or where I went. I just know where I wound up."

He tightened his arms around her, pulling her against his chest. "I looked for you on the streets," he admitted. "I don't know how you survived on your own."

She smiled. "I guess maybe there's a benefit to being crazy. No one messed with me. No one really noticed me…unless I was buying booze or drugs from them."

"Irina—"

"I told you I was a mess," she said. "The only way I could block out the voices was if I blacked out." Her lips lifted again, her smile strained. "Sweet oblivion."

"Irina, I'm so sorry."

"It's over now." Irina waved off his concern. "I'm stronger now."

"You were stronger *then*." She'd had to be to survive that life. "You just didn't know it."

She reached up and kissed his chin. "I know it now."

Sharply focused, her dark eyes glistened with determination. Dread pressed against Ty's heart; he was done butting up against her strong will. If he had to, he'd drag her to the penthouse.

Smiling again, that sad smile, she shook her head, silently arguing with his thought. "I know where my mother was when he killed her. The snow globe reminded me. She was at the last place we were all together. The last place we were a family."

His dread increased. She lifted her chin with pride and even more determination, intent on a plan she'd concocted, a plan that had the hairs lifting on his nape and his guts twisting with fear. "Irina—"

She pulled free of his arms, taking the sheet with her, clasped to her breasts, as she left the bed they'd shared so briefly. "Tell my sisters I'll meet them there."

He struggled for patience, hoping to reason with her. "Irina, I don't have my cell."

She picked up the phone beside the bed and handed it to him. He pressed the cordless to his ear, but no dial tone rang out. "It's been disconnected."

"Then you'll have to go to them," she said, her voice soft with patience as she tried his. "You can tell them where to meet me."

"Us," he corrected her, rolling out of bed. "You're not going to Armaya without me."

"Armaya?"

"It's Gypsy for *curse* and the name of the town where you all grew up when your mother wasn't on the road with you." He studied her through narrowed eyes. Had she just tricked him? "I thought you remembered."

"I just remembered the cornfield."

From her globe. That's why she'd had it; it had probably reminded her of home. The only one she'd ever really known, the only place she'd ever really been accepted.

"Come with me to the penthouse," he said as he walked up behind her where she stood in front of her open closet doors. Deciding what to wear or if the clothes were even hers?

There were parts of his life he'd wanted to forget, but they'd stayed there, buried in his mind, ready to be resurrected should he dig for them. He couldn't imagine not being able to remember...if he wanted to. Even when he hadn't wanted, he'd remembered….

"No," she said as she ran her hands along the sleeves of shirts and sweaters sticking out of the closet.

"You and Ariel and Elena can ride up to Armaya together," he said. The way they'd ridden away from it, in the back of a sheriff's car that had brought them to the closest city with child-protective services. Barrett. They'd never left.

She shook her head, tangling her dark curls around her bare shoulders. "No. I want to meet at the spot where she died. I want to bury her remains, Ty. I need to give her peace." Tears streaked down her face. "If I'm ever going to have any peace myself."

"Irina…" He wrapped an arm around her, pulling her tight against him.

"I hated her for so long. Resented her. Until the day she died." She sniffled, smothering a sob, then murmured, "When Roarke was killing her, she didn't plead for her life, Ty. She pleaded for *ours*."

"Ariel and Elena believe she didn't fight to keep her children because she was trying to protect you." God, Irina must have thought her own mother didn't want her. Then, because of her telepathy, the Bowerses hadn't. No wonder she feared meeting her sisters—she feared their rejection.

Her voice soft, Irina murmured, "She tried protecting us…with her last breath."

He leaned closer, brushing a kiss across her bare shoulder, trying to offer comfort even though he still didn't know how. "Your mother could see the future, like Elena can. She knew that someday the vendetta would be resurrected, the witch hunt would start up again."

"She knew he was coming for her," Irina agreed, pulling away from him, refusing his comfort. "She knew…so she went home. To Armaya. Have my sisters meet me there."

"Irina, this is a bad idea…." He didn't even know the extent of her plan, but he suspected it put her in danger. Because so few other people ever had, Irina didn't care about herself.

"Your clothes are in the dryer," she said as she pulled jeans and a sweater from the closet. "It should be done now."

"I can't leave you alone." His gut clenched as he rebelled at the thought of leaving her on her own again. "Come with me to a pay phone."

"We both know a phone call won't be good enough to convince your friends to go to Armaya."

"So come with me to the penthouse," he said. "We'll all drive up together."

She patted his cheek, then rubbed her hand

over the beard on his jaw. "Ty, I thought you trusted me."

He wanted to. "It's Roarke I don't trust."

"I'll be safe," she assured him. "I have the charm now."

Chapter 9

I had the charm. That was the only reason Ty left her. And she'd promised to wait for him to return before she headed to Armaya. He wished he could read her mind. He wished he knew if he'd misplaced his trust in her.

"God, Ty, what the hell were you thinking!" David shouted at him, his agitation apparent in the jerky way he paced the marble floor of the penthouse living room. "First you don't pick up your phone—you could have died in that fire. Now you leave her alone—"

"She's not in any danger. Roarke doesn't even

know we're alive," Ty pointed out from where he sat on the couch next to the glass-topped coffee table, his leg throbbing too badly for him to try to keep up with his friend. He'd pushed himself these last few days, physically and emotionally. He'd felt more pain and more joy than he'd ever considered himself capable of feeling.

Because of Irina.

David shook his head. "He knows—"

"You're saying he has some special gift now?" Ty scoffed. He refused to accept that there was anything special or supernatural about Roarke. If he did, he might have to consider that they wouldn't ever be rid of the madman.

"All he had to do was listen to the news," David said. "Every station reported on the fire."

Ty's guts twisted. *Damn it all.*

"Everybody in Barrett knows you escaped that fire, you and the woman who was staying with you," David said, then he lowered his voice and his gaze caught Ty's and held, full of questions, "in *that* house?"

"Nobody would look for us there."

"I sure as hell wouldn't have," David admitted. He knew how much Ty had hated the house where he'd grown up—where he almost hadn't had the chance to grow up. "But that house is gone." From his tone, he felt its incineration as overdue as Ty had. "So where is she now?"

"She remembered where she'd been living when she…" He couldn't say that she'd lost it; she'd just been managing the best she could. Alone. She'd protected herself even without the charm. She'd stayed hidden from Roarke—and them—for a long time.

"Is that where she is?" David asked.

Ty nodded. "Her apartment."

"You really left her alone?" Ariel asked, staring up at him from where she sat on the black leather sofa. "You spend all this time searching for her for *us*. And you don't bring her here?" Her turquoise eyes were wide with disbelief and disillusionment.

He'd let her down. It wasn't the first time. When once her disappointment would have filled him with regret, he felt barely a twinge. Irina was the one he was determined to not let down, to not let get hurt.

"Her name's not on the lease." The way his had been on the deed that Roarke had no doubt tracked down. "And she has the charm."

Elena's blond head bobbed as she nodded. "She'll be fine, Ariel," she assured her sister, wrapping her arm around Ariel's shoulders as she sat next to her on the couch. "Don't worry." But then she lifted her pale gaze to Ty, impaling him with her angry glare.

"She will be fine," Ty insisted, trying to convince himself as much as them. "She's stronger than you all think she is." Stronger than even she thought she was.

"She was living on the streets," David reminded him. "She was homeless. Destitute. Out of her mind when they brought her in to the psych ward. You don't think I checked everything out?"

He always did.

"But you didn't meet her." He didn't know her the way Ty did, intimately both physically and emotionally. She'd been part of him for so long, part of those long-buried memories.

"Whose fault is it that I haven't met her?" David shot back at him.

"All right," Joseph Dolce spoke up from where he sat next to Elena, his arm around her shoulders. "Let's all calm down. Why doesn't she want to come here?"

Ariel's eyes shimmered with unshed tears. "She doesn't want to meet us?"

"Does she even know who we are?" Elena asked. "She was so young when they took us all away from Mother."

"She knows you," Ty assured them. "She can hear all your thoughts. She knows *everything* that's happened. She's heard you."

"And him?" Elena asked, her pale eyes damp with fear and dread. "She's heard Roarke?"

He nodded. He couldn't imagine the thoughts she'd heard, the evil intent as hatred and madness controlled the man. She was far stronger than even he'd given her credit for to have survived with her sanity.

"Oh God…" Ariel's breath shuddered out. "That must have been so horrible for her."

"And she was all alone," Elena added.

"She's alone now," David pointed out.

Ty's anger rose beyond his control. They were wasting his time, keeping him away from her. "Then shut the hell up and let me say what I have to so I can get back to her."

David's dark eyes flickered with surprise, his chin dropping. "Ty—"

"Let him talk," Joseph advised, ever the CEO.

Ty ignored the men, focusing instead on the two women sitting so close together on the couch. Irina should be with them instead of alone as she'd been so much of her life. "Irina knows where your mother died, in the cornfield in Armaya. She wants to meet you both there, with the charms. She wants to find and bury your mother's remains."

"No!" Elena shouted, jumping up from the couch. "She can't go there!"

Elena's panic was contagious. Ty's heart hurt as if something pressed on his chest. Obviously she knew something he didn't, something only she could know—about the future. "Why can't she go there?"

Elena's voice trembled as she related her latest vision. "*He* takes her there. That's where he kills her, burning her at the stake like he did our mother. I've seen it, Ty. I've seen him *kill* her."

Fear flowed through Ty's veins, quickening his pulse. He drew in a deep breath, reminding himself that Elena's visions didn't always come to pass. Roarke hadn't gotten Irina in the alley, as her older sister had envisioned. She'd been strong enough to escape him then. She would escape him again.

He'd make certain of that.

"You've had that vision before, the one of her burning, like Mama," Ariel remembered. Her entire body trembled as if she'd been out in the cold too long.

David stopped his restless pacing to pull her up from the couch and into his arms, offering her the warmth and comfort of his love.

Things Ty had thought he could never give anyone. Until he'd met Irina. But she deserved better. She deserved a man who wouldn't snap and hurt her someday, who didn't have so much rage inside him.

He focused on Elena, urging her, "Tell me about your vision."

"I had another one last night, after the one about the house fire," Elena said. "And as you asked me, Ty, I paid attention to all the details. So this time I saw where she was…in the cornfield."

"That's where she wants to meet you," Ty reminded them.

"She was alone, Ty," Elena said, tears streaming down her face. "We didn't get to her in time. She was all alone but for Roarke."

Irina walked around the apartment, anxious for Ty's return. She'd only been with him a few days, but already she missed him. Already she'd grown unused to being alone when that was how she'd spent so much of her life.

Except here. She'd had a roommate. Briefly. She knew the crystals and herbs were Maria's, not hers. The girl had been odd but accepting—when so few people had ever accepted Irina as she was.

Ty accepted her.

Would her sisters? Nerves fluttered in her stomach over the thought of seeing them again. She didn't want to disappoint them as she had so many others.

Restless, she paced around the living room,

touching each knickknack on the shelves and the mantel. Then she turned her attention to the coffee table, where the crystals were strewn across the tarot cards. She lifted them away, the stones cool against her skin unlike the charm that held so much warmth. She revealed the cards beneath the crystals; a few of them were faceup. One picture was of a burning tower, two people jumping from blazing windows.

She shivered, rubbing her arms over the sleeves of her red cashmere sweater. Despite how many times she'd washed it, smoke still clung to her hair and burned in her nostrils.

She focused on the card next to the tower. A man rode atop a white horse, a knight, a cape whipping behind him as he brandished a sword. She brushed her fingertip over the knight. Her warrior? Ty? The card next to that one also featured a knight atop a white horse, but this one was a skeleton.

She shuddered in recognition of the death card. Although no fire burned in the hearth, she walked back over to the fireplace, hugging herself. She knew what the death card meant.

Even though she'd never used the cards, they were so familiar to her. Did she remember Maria reading them? Or her mother twenty years ago when she'd supported her family as a fortune-teller?

Despite her gift, Mama hadn't always told the truth, though. She'd explained how people were happier when they didn't know the truth.

Had she been happy? Ever?

Irina picked up the snow globe from the shelf and shook it, mesmerized by the details, by the way the stalks trembled when the crows floated down onto them and the scarecrow. But then, despite her concentration on the globe, despite the sunlight glaring brightly in the room, darkness enveloped her. Only small bits of red glowing in a sea of black.

Ty's blood again. She was certain of it because she heard Roarke's thoughts.

I knew he'd come here...if I waited. He switched vehicles, ditching the Mustang reported stolen from the house near the one I burned. He's smart. He escaped me there. He won't escape me this time. I'll wait until he leaves the penthouse and comes back down here. The security guards won't follow him like they do the women. No one will be watching him but me.

"No!" The protest burst from Irina's lips like a curse. "Not Ty."

She'd done it once before, when they were kids—she'd gotten inside his head. He'd heard her. He'd been unconscious, half-dead, but he'd heard her. So she squeezed her eyes shut and concentrated hard. But she couldn't hear a single one of his thoughts. All she felt was a rage that had her shaking. Was it Ty's? Or Roarke's? Or hers?

She couldn't let Donovan Roarke hurt Ty. She had to do something. But when she grabbed the phone, the dull silence reminded her that the service had been cut off. Then next to the phone she glimpsed the pewter moon. She picked up the charm, her fingers warming from the metal even while they trembled with fear.

She pushed the charm into the pocket of her jeans, but the glint of something else metal on the coffee table caught her attention. A key chain, from which dangled a keyless-entry remote.

She had a car. She ran from the apartment so quickly that she barely slammed the door shut behind herself. Then she clicked the horn button so the Saturn blared a greeting at her. Now all she had to do was get to Ty before Donovan Roarke did.

Anger gripped Ty, tensing every muscle so that his jaw and his neck ached. He was mad at himself. Just as he had on his last day on the job, he'd lost his objectivity. He'd gotten emotionally involved, and if he didn't hurry, he might lose Irina again.

Permanently. Ignoring the pain throbbing in his leg, he rushed through the parking garage, intent on getting back to Irina, on making sure she stayed safe.

Despite their resentment toward how he'd handled her, his friends trusted him to protect her. To make sure she got to Armaya unharmed. He wouldn't let them down again.

But what happened once they got there, to the place where their mother had been viciously murdered? How safe would any of the sisters be then?

He couldn't imagine their heartbreak, only his own if something happened to Irina. How had she come to mean so much to him?

What was *he* to *her?* A rescuer? A bodyguard? With his past, that was really all he could be, so he would make certain he didn't fail her. What happened to him after they went to Armaya? Would he turn her over to the protection of her sisters and walk away from her?

He had to; with her found, he had to focus on Roarke, on stopping the psychopath's killing rampage. The rage surged inside him again. If he had to *kill* to stop the killing, he would. Whatever was necessary to protect Irina and her sisters...

His hand shaking with anger, the keys to his

second vehicle slipped through his fingers. He'd ditched the stolen Mustang this morning after leaving Irina's apartment and had picked up his winter beater, an old Suburban. He'd probably need the four-wheel drive in Armaya. In the cornfield. Unless he could talk Irina out of meeting her sisters there.

Just as he bent over to pick up his keys, shots rang out, and the glass in the vehicle behind him burst, showering fragments over the cement like sparks from a firework.

"Goddamn it," he uttered as his heart slammed against his ribs. He'd been vigilant when he'd left Irina's and at his apartment when he'd picked up the Suburban. He'd been certain no one had been following him. Roarke had been here instead, waiting. Lying in ambush.

But maybe Roarke had walked into the trap. David had increased security around the building, protecting it, as Ty had told Irina, as if the skyscraper housing his business and home was Fort Knox. But the millionaire considered Ariel far more precious than any amount of money. Security had to have heard the shots; they'd be coming soon.

Ty stayed hunkered down against the side of the black van beside which he'd dropped his keys. He reached again for the metal ring, which had fallen next to the running board. As he did, something warm and wet plopped on the back of his hand. He glanced down at the droplet, stark crimson against his skin.

Damn, had Roarke hit him? Or was it some glass, like the other night? Maybe the adrenaline pouring through him kept him from feeling the pain. But when he picked up his keys, they were wet and sticky, too. He leaned out and peered under the running board at the blood pooling on the cement. Then he glanced up at the van, where a man's shattered skull leaned against the driver's window.

No, security wouldn't be helping him out. Roarke had already gotten to them. *Son of a bitch!*

He held his breath, listening for any sound to give away Roarke's location. Then the man himself spoke. "You can't hide from me, McIntyre. You're not a witch like the women. You have no special powers. If I'm not mistaken, you don't even have a gun."

They'd taken it when they'd taken his badge. The only gun he'd had was his service revolver, but he'd been told to not carry another until he was cleared in the suspect's death. Since he wouldn't have been able to get a permit for a new one, he should have gotten a gun off the street, the way he had for David when his best friend had asked for one to protect Ariel. Ty had already broken a lot of laws to protect Irina; he should have broken another.

Right now *he* needed the protection, though. Since he didn't have a weapon, he'd have to use his wits. Roarke was waiting for him to answer back so he could find out if and where he'd moved.

Ty needed to move; there was no sense in waiting for help that wouldn't come. Staying low, he slipped between cars, heading toward where he'd parked the Suburban. Maybe Roarke was waiting there for him, but that was a chance he had to take. As he passed close to a luxury car, an alarm sounded, sensitive to the brush of his body against the driver's side. Shots rang out, reverberating off the walls of the cement building, while bullets dented metal and broke glass, bits of which rained down on Ty as he ran.

More shots fired, the burst of gunpowder like an explosion in the enclosed parking structure. Bullets glanced off mirrors and metal near Ty. Bent over to make himself a smaller target, he didn't notice the grate missing until his foot slipped inside it. Cement scraped his ankle, tearing skin, and pain jarred his bad leg as he sprawled across the ground. A groan tore from his lips before he could bite it back. He dragged himself up. But it was too late.

The cold metal of a gun barrel pressed against his temple. "You are accident-prone," Roarke tsked, the amusement in his voice telling Ty who had removed the grate, probably one of several he'd pulled loose.

"This is your first mistake, Roarke," Ty said, hoping to disarm the man by both praising and undermining the killer. Stroking his ego at the same time he chipped away at it, making Roarke doubt himself.

"This is *my* mistake? I don't think so," the madman scoffed.

"You should have let me go," Ty said. "I could have led you right back to Irina."

Roarke laughed. "You may be a klutz, McIntyre, but you're no fool. You would have caught my tail. And you would have lost me." He sighed. "It's too bad, really, that I have to kill you. You were a good police officer."

"Unlike you."

"I was too good. Too good for the force. I had a higher calling. And now I know what it is." His voice burgeoning with self-importance, he continued, "To vanquish witchcraft. To destroy all the witches."

Ty swallowed the curse burning his tongue; he

didn't want Roarke pulling the trigger yet. His fingers wrapped around the steel grate the madman had left next to the drain hole. "Then why me? Like you said, I'm no witch."

"You're in my way. Like so many others. Like your friend Koster and that Dolce guy." Hatred dripped from his rabid voice. "You just keep getting in my way, messing up my plans. I can't have that."

Ty tried to shake his head, but the barrel held him firm. "You're not going to find Irina now—"

"I won't have to." The barrel pressed harder against Ty's temple. "You need to make a call. Oh, that's right—you probably lost your cell in the fire. Use mine." With his free hand, he pressed a phone to Ty's ear.

"I can't call her. She has no phone," he explained, hoping Roarke wasn't too crazy to recognize the truth.

"Don't you believe in her powers?" Roarke taunted him. "Don't you believe that she can read minds? That she knows exactly how much fear you're feeling now and that she's already on her way to *save* you?"

Dread pressed on his heart. Ty did believe in Irina's gift, her telepathy. Did she know what the madman had planned?

Did she know that Ty didn't want her to risk her life to try to stop him? He closed his eyes, concentrating hard on transmitting his thoughts to her. *Don't come here. It's what he wants. Stay away, Irina.*

"I believe," Ty said. But he hoped to hell Irina couldn't find a way to get to Koster Tower. Because he knew no matter how loudly she heard his thoughts, she wouldn't listen to him. She wouldn't stay away. She was too damned stubborn. "Don't *you* believe in her ability, Roarke?"

"Her witchcraft," the lunatic corrected him with a snort of disgust as he punched in numbers on the cell phone. "She bewitched you, McIntyre, putting you under her spell. Was she worth your life?"

Yes.

"If you really believed she was a witch, you wouldn't be calling her," Ty pointed out, trying to reason with the psycho. "You wouldn't need to."

How could Roarke call her when she didn't have a phone? He pressed the Send button, and ringing emanated from the phone. Ty sucked in a breath, waiting to see if the psycho had found a way to contact Irina.

But a deep voice answered. "Barber, I've been trying to reach you. The desk called with reports of shots fired in the parking garage. What the hell's going on—"

Roarke had taken the security guard's phone after he killed him. Ty broke into his friend's tirade with, "David—"

The madman pulled the phone back. "If you want to see your friend again, Koster, you and Dolce will join us in the parking garage."

David's voice filtered down to Ty. "You son of a bitch, you killed him!"

"Your security guard, yes," he gloated. "Your friend, not yet." Then he cocked the barrel of the gun held against Ty's temple.

If Ty didn't do something quick, he'd be no protection for Irina, no protection against whatever the killer had planned for his friends.

He had to act.

Or die.

Chapter 10

"David, it's a trap!" Ty shouted as he swung the heavy metal grate. The steel struck Roarke's arm, knocking the gun free from his grip. Then Ty swung again, aiming at the man's head. But the blow glanced off Roarke's arm, lifted in defense as his fist jammed into Ty's jaw. Pain radiating throughout his face, Ty fell onto the cement and rolled on his side, trying to pull himself back up.

Roarke regained his feet first and kicked Ty in the stomach, knocking his breath out between his teeth in a painful hiss. When Roarke kicked again, Ty was ready and caught his foot, pulling the madman down beside him. Roarke groaned as his body hit the concrete.

All the people he'd killed, all of those he'd terrorized and hurt...their faces rolled through Ty's mind. And the rage always simmering deep inside him snapped his control. He grabbed Donovan Roarke, holding his collar with one hand as he pummeled the man's face with the other. The skin on Ty's knuckles cracked, blood oozing out of the cuts. But he didn't notice his pain.

Roarke tried to hit back, throwing punches at Ty's face. He tried to hold him off, extending his arms and pushing against Ty's shoulders. But Roarke couldn't shake him off. Anger ruled Ty, increasing his strength.

But madness infused Roarke's ailing body with strength, too, like an addict out of his mind on drugs. During his career, Ty had fought with more than his share of both men and women tripping out. Then, he hadn't had at stake what he did now—the lives of his friends and the woman he...

He and Roarke grappled, rolling across the cement, hitting up against cars as they struck each other. Knowing his weakness, beyond caring about himself, Ty head-butted Roarke. The guy's eyes rolled back, only the red-streaked whites showing. Then Ty's hands closed around Roarke's throat, the way his father's hands used to do to his throat.

And he squeezed.

"No!" He heard her thought even before the vehicle she drove, a little red SUV, rolled to a stop across the ramp from him.

"Ty!" she screamed his name.

He could barely hear her voice now, let alone his thoughts. Rage rushed through his head, roaring in his ears. He couldn't hear her. What was she thinking? Don't become Roarke? Don't become a killer?

It was too late. He had already killed. More than once in the line of duty. He'd been cleared all but the last time, but still he'd always wondered…had he had to kill or had he wanted to kill?

Something struck the back of Ty's head, metal clashing with hair and skin and bone. Black spots swam before his eyes as he struggled to maintain consciousness. He fought against the darkness; he couldn't leave Irina alone with Roarke, couldn't leave her at a madman's mercy.

Blinded with pain, he reached around. Roarke had the grate—that was what he'd struck him with—but the gun lay around somewhere. He scraped his palms across the concrete, searching. He'd no more than grabbed the weapon when he was knocked back against a car. He blinked to clear his vision, but instead of Roarke coming at him—or at Irina where she sat in her vehicle, laying on her horn—he was running away, his footsteps pounding against the cement.

Ty tried to lift the gun, tried to site it at Roarke's retreating back. But Roarke's image wavered. Ty focused on Irina instead.

Had Roarke hit her? Was that why her horn blared, echoing off the walls of the parking garage? Had he hurt her? Had he *shot* her?

Ty was sure he'd never lost consciousness. Or lost track of the gun he grasped tight in his bleeding hand.

"Bomb! He set a bomb!" she screamed at Ty through her open window. "Hurry up!"

But he lay crumpled against the side the car, struggling for strength when just a short time ago he'd had so much. But then rage had driven him. His head reeled, and as dizziness washed over him, his limbs weakened even more.

Irina vaulted out of her car. "Ty, there's a bomb. We have to run."

Through eyes blurred with pain Ty watched Irina start toward him. She'd only run a few yards across the distance separating them when a van careened around the corner, bearing down on her.

* * *

Die, witch, die! Irina heard Roarke's thoughts before the squeal of tires as the van headed straight toward her. She froze. If she ran toward Ty, he might get run over, too. But if she didn't move—

Something hard slammed into her, knocking her to the concrete. Then she and Ty, limbs entwined, rolled. The van passed, the squealing tires just missing them. She buried her face in Ty's neck, pressing a kiss of gratitude and relief to his skin. The metallic taste of blood clung to her lips, sticky and sweet. "Ty, you're hurt."

He groaned but managed to pull himself to his feet and lift her off the concrete. "Bomb?"

Urgency pressed on her heart again. "Get in," she cried, pulling him toward her running Saturn Vue. "He set a bomb in your vehicle."

She jumped into the driver's seat, he the passenger's side. He turned toward her, his face pale beneath the smears of dirt and blood streaking his cheek and jaw. Her heart clenched over the damage Roarke's fists had inflicted on Ty. Pain reeled through her head and radiated throughout her body. He was in the same shape he'd been in the first time she'd met him, when he'd been a boy hovering on the brink of death. "Ty, you're hurt." Badly.

Blood matted his hair and saturated the collar of his T-shirt. He had a head wound. She had to get him to safety, then to a hospital.

His voice a weak rasp of pain, Ty murmured, "He lured David and Joseph down here. We have to warn them."

She gunned the engine. "There's no time—"

"We have to drive through the garage and look for *them*. They're looking for *me*."

She didn't have to hear what he was thinking to know that he could never leave a friend in danger, especially if the friend was in danger because of *him*. But at the moment she didn't care about saving his friends, she only cared about him. "Ty…"

He curled his hand around her arm. "Your sisters might have come with them." *Knowing how stubborn both women were, he was certain that they had.*

Irina's pulse quickened as she realized her sisters could be in danger…that they could be killed before she'd had the chance to meet up with them again. Regret hung heavy around her shoulders because it was *her* fault she'd not seen them yet and because, once again, Ty knew them so much better than she did. He knew that they wouldn't hesitate over walking into a madman's trap in order to save a friend and that no one could stop them once they'd made up their minds.

Roarke would be furious; no one was following his plan. He'd planned to set the bomb, to use Ty to lure his friends down from the penthouse. He'd wanted to kill the men with the bomb, not the witches.

He'd underestimated her. He hadn't believed she cared enough about Ty to come to his aid. But she cared so much about him she hesitated over warning her sisters.

"I don't think we have enough time to look for them," she said, her protest weak as she careened around the floors of the parking garage, driving just slow enough that they could scream at anyone they saw to leave. Now.

Her hands trembling on the wheel, she turned toward the man bleeding in the passenger seat, the headrest of the gray cloth seat turning dark with his blood. "We're putting ourselves in jeopardy, Ty."

"Roarke did that," he said, his voice thick with bitterness and pain.

"We have to get out of here before the bomb goes off." She had a feeling Roarke might have timed it tight, unwilling to take the chance of Ty escaping him, of Ty escaping death, yet again.

* * *

From the alley across the street, Roarke watched the entrance to the parking garage, only taking his gaze away to glance in the rearview mirror. His face reflected back at him, distorted like a fun-house mirror. His skin had swelled and reddened from McIntyre's fists. Blood trickled from a cut on his forehead; he blinked the drops back from his eye.

"Damn that interfering son of a bitch!"

He couldn't wait until the ex-cop died, buried beneath the rubble along with the other trouble-makers, leaving Roarke free to carry out his family's legacy, to finish the witch hunt. With the men, one of the witches would die. The bomb wasn't a ritualistic way of killing, but he didn't care.

He needed the men gone; they'd derailed his plans too many times. The witches, without the protection of the bewitched men, would be easy to get to, easy to kill.

So he'd called up one of his Army buddies, an explosives expert who'd talked him through how to make the dirty bomb. Finding the C4 had been the tough thing, but he'd found another buddy who owed him a favor, like so many others, for keeping his secrets. That guy had found him enough of the explosive to blow up the parking garage's main support. With it gone, the whole thing should collapse.

Onto McIntyre, his two friends and the witch who'd tried to save them… What had happened to the wreck who'd cowered in the alley, hiding from him, hiding from her gift?

He'd counted on her being too scared to really try to help McIntyre. He'd expected she'd call the men instead, further luring them to the parking ramp. But he should have learned by now that the witches didn't do what he wanted.

They were hard to kill. Until now.

All he had to do was wait. He glanced at his wristwatch, the crystal broken from his fight with McIntyre. But the hands kept moving toward the appointed time that the bomb would go off. Toward the time when there'd be no one standing between him and the remaining witches.

Irina blinked, fighting her way out of the black hatred of Donovan Roarke's thoughts. "We can't waste any more time looking for them, Ty. The bomb is going to go off any minute."

And Roarke was waiting for the explosion from his front-row seat, ready to gloat. An explosion wasn't a ritualistic way of killing a witch—but then, he hadn't intended to kill any of the witches in the explosion. *She* was an accident. She just hoped her sisters wouldn't be, too.

She kept driving, chanting their names in her head. Ariel. Elena.

Ty had to be wrong; they hadn't come down here to save him. They were up in the penthouse, safe.

They had to be.

"Over there, slow down," Ty commanded. "I see David and Joseph." He opened the door to the Vue, but Irina caught his arm, holding him inside, unwilling to let him take even a step away from her.

So he shouted at his friends, "Bomb!"

Irina didn't watch for the men's reactions. She'd just noticed two women hunched behind a dark-colored car. They hid near a bank of elevators and a stairwell, certain to have escape routes. Even in the dimly lit garage, Irina managed a good look at them. A redhead and a blonde, aged twenty years from the little girls she remembered. Faintly.

Her hand shaking, she pressed the button that rolled down her window. Her first contact with her sisters in over twenty years was a single word, screamed. "Bomb!"

The men sprinted behind the Vue, hurling themselves toward the women they loved, pulling them up and running with them toward the stairwell.

"Step on it!" Ty yelled as he slammed shut the passenger door again.

After one last longing glance at where the stairwell door closed behind her sisters, Irina pressed on the accelerator, racing the Vue toward the exit. Even though the guard shack neared, she didn't lift her foot from the accelerator. She blew right through the wooden barrier. The front bumper snapped the beam in pieces that skittered across the pavement. Wood splinters rolled across the hood and struck the windshield but didn't block her vision. She careened into traffic, other drivers' horns blaring in protest.

Ty gripped the door and the console, his dark blue eyes wide with surprise as he turned to her. "I didn't know you could drive like this," he murmured.

"Neither did I," Irina remarked.

Then the world exploded. All the windows shattered, glass imploding on them as pieces of vehicles and cement burst into the street just behind them. Plastic and jagged chunks of metal rolled across the asphalt as if chasing after them.

"Keep driving!" he shouted over the deafening noise. He reached across and covered her hand on the wheel, helping her steer the vehicle through the cloud of dust and debris that was more blinding than her telepathy.

"We have to go back. We have to check on them," she pleaded, trying to twist the wheel back toward the parking complex.

"No!" Ty protested, strong enough to wrest control of the vehicle away from her. "We can't go back. Roarke's still around there. He's waiting. He's watching."

"You have his gun." She pointed toward the weapon lying where he'd dropped it on the floorboards.

"And you don't think he'll have another? You can't underestimate Donovan Roarke." He spoke from experience, his voice thick with frustration.

From having spent time in the killer's head, she knew the truth in what Ty said. She couldn't argue with him. She also couldn't underestimate Roarke the way he'd underestimated her.

"He's desperate, Irina. Unpredictable. If we go back," he pointed out, "we're at his mercy."

"Donovan Roarke has no mercy," she corrected him, her heart thumping with dread as she considered all those who might have been harmed in the explosion in addition to her sisters.

"No, he doesn't. That's why we have to keep driving…." *Because he was too weak to fight him again.*

"Ty? Are you all right?"

He nodded, his head lolling weakly on his neck. "Yeah, yeah, I'm fine...."

She didn't believe him, but she knew he wouldn't tell her the truth about himself. "Are *they* all right?" she asked. "I need to know if my sisters…"

Had survived. But she couldn't say the words aloud; she could barely think them.

"Yes, they're all right," Ty insisted above the roar of the wind whistling through all the broken windows. "David and Joseph would have made sure nothing happened to them."

Had they gotten far enough away from the explosion? Would the stairwell prove any protection or a tomb for their broken bodies?

Panic rose, threatening to send Irina back to that place inside herself where she'd retreated in the alley, where she'd lost all sense of reality. She lifted her chin, struggling against the despair. She was stronger now, too strong to fall completely apart.

Had her last chance at a reunion with her sisters been that one word she'd screamed at them? Why had she been so stubborn, why had she resisted meeting them, when now she might never have the chance? Her pride, damn it; she'd let her pride hold her back, worried that they would be disappointed in the choices she'd made, in the life she'd led since she was separated from them.

A sob bubbled up, but she swallowed it down, fighting to keep her composure. She had to stay strong because, in the seat next to her, Ty was slipping away…the blood seeping from his head wound dripped from his hair and had soaked his shirt so completely that the cotton clung to him.

"Ty!" she yelled above the noise. "Ty, look at me."

His navy-blue eyes rolled back in his head as he slumped in the seat, unconscious.

Or dead?

Had he stayed alive only long enough to save her again?

Chapter 11

"I'm okay," Ty insisted as he fumbled the motel key into the lock and thrust open the door to the room they'd rented just an hour south of Armaya, Michigan.

He'd told her the name of the town was Gypsy for *curse*. Would that prove true for them? Was she making a mistake in making them all meet where her mother had been murdered?

She hoped her sisters were alive to make the meeting.

Fear and panic gripped her, reaction from the

explosion setting in, so that she trembled. Her teeth chattered as cold chilled her to the bone.

"I want to take you to an emergency room," she said, focusing on Ty, "get you an X-ray. I'm sure you have a concussion. You passed out, Ty."

But thankfully for only a moment. If he'd been out longer, she might have fallen apart. She certainly wouldn't have been able to keep driving, as he'd insisted she do. With all the windows out, they couldn't take her Saturn to Armaya. So they'd switched for a cheap car they found for sale along the road. He had a lot of cash on him, enough for the car and for the motel room they'd rented. "Cash?" she'd asked.

"We're fugitives," he'd reminded her in a whisper, which was why she hadn't been able to take him to the hospital for the X-ray and stitches he desperately needed. He'd had to explain all that though; she hadn't been *listening* to him.

She was too exhausted, both physically and emotionally, to tap into anyone's thoughts at the moment, even her own. "We need to call Ariel and Elena," she insisted, "to make sure they're all right."

"You don't know?" Ty asked, lifting his scarred eyebrow as she passed through the door in front of him.

She barely noticed the threadbare commercial

carpet and the dingy beige walls of the little room, unconcerned about where she was. Last time she'd felt like that, she'd wound up living behind a Dumpster.

Shaking her head, she admitted, "I'm too scared. If they were hurt and I never really got to talk to them…"

Strong arms wrapped around her, pulling her close to his hard chest. "They're okay."

"How do you know?"

"Because I know them."

And she didn't. He didn't think it; he didn't have to. She didn't know her sisters because she'd hidden away from them, even after she'd come out of the alley. Damn her pride, her fear of rejection. What did it matter whether or not they loved her?

"They have to be okay," he maintained. "They have the charms."

"You're so certain that they can protect us, that they can stop this witch hunt?" The crescent moon was still in her pocket, warm against her hip. Was it the reason they'd survived the explosion?

"I believe that the witch hunt might be stopped when all three charms are reunited. Your mother sent postcards to her sisters with symbols of the charms on them. She circled all three together. Ariel thinks it means—"

"Nothing. It means nothing. None of it. None of it has a purpose. People are dying." Maybe her sisters were dead now, lying beneath a pile of rubble. The charms be damned. She had no faith in their protection. No faith in them or her own power that failed her when she needed it most. She needed to hear her sisters now, to know that they were all right.

And even though he stood before her, her arms wrapped tight around him, she wasn't yet sure that Ty was all right. He'd lost so much blood. "You almost died today, Ty."

Or worse. He'd almost killed...with his bare hands. All his fears of being his father's son were justified.

She stepped back, and the thought flitted through his head that she'd heard him and was repulsed. But then she lifted her hands, pressing her palms against his face. Holding his gaze steady with hers, she insisted, "You are *not* your father. You will *never* be your father."

"I have his rage, his propensity for violence. It's in me, Irina," he said, his voice full of dread and self-condemnation. "You can read my thoughts— you know it's true."

And she'd feared him because of those thoughts, because of that rage...until she'd met him. Now she knew his tenderness and generosity. He controlled the anger, but he couldn't control his selflessness. "I know you're true, Ty. You're real."

"And you don't know what else is?"

Maybe he'd gotten inside her head, the way she'd gotten into his.

"The explosion. The vendetta. It all seems unreal." She rose up, pressing her breasts to his chest. "But you." She pressed her lips to his, then murmured, "But this."

His hands tangled in her hair as he first held her mouth to his, then pulled her away. "Irina…"

"I'm afraid, Ty." And she needed his arms around her, holding her close against his beating heart.

She'd been strong on her own when she'd found the parking garage, when she'd found him, when she'd driven them to safety. Now she wanted someone to hold her; she didn't want to be alone anymore.

Her breath—that she'd probably been holding since he'd passed out—shuddered out of her. "I keep thinking I'm going to wake up. That it's all been a dream."

"It's real," he assured her, but from the grimace twisting his handsome face, he remembered the bad things, not the lovemaking. Or maybe he really didn't feel the way about her that she did about him.

He probably couldn't. No one else had ever been able to love her.

"I keep thinking I'm going to wake up," she repeated, then continued, "and I'll be in that alley again."

The memory of the Dumpster, the stench clinging to it, to her, flitted through her mind while the cold from the asphalt, from the brick building at her back, seeped into her bones again, chilling her. Even held close to the warmth of his body, she shivered. "I keep thinking I'll be alone."

"You're not alone."

Now.

She wasn't sure which of them thought that, but it didn't matter since it was true. For the moment, *now* and Ty were all that mattered.

She caught his hand and tugged him toward the bathroom. "Let me clean you up. I'm sure you need stitches."

"It stopped bleeding."

Although he didn't betray it to her by thought or expression, she felt his worry for his friends. He was just as concerned about her sisters and their fiancés as she was. Did his worry for Ariel run deeper than his concern for the others, than his feelings for *her?*

She pushed aside the jealousy and resentment,

hating that such selfish feelings could creep into her concern. He'd assured her before they'd made love the first time that only friendship existed between him and Ariel. But maybe she envied that, too, his deep relationships with these people who were supposed to be closer to her. She was family, but she'd been cut off from them for so long she wasn't sure how to reach out to them anymore…or even if she could.

"Your wound needs to be cleaned," she said, focusing on the person she could touch, the person she usually couldn't stop touching. They both needed to be cleansed—of the worries and the scars from their pasts.

Ty followed her across the threadbare motel room carpet to the bathroom. He leaned against the sink while she ran water in the tub. His navy gaze studied her, unsettling her with his intensity. When she wanted to know most what he was thinking, he shut her out.

Her heart lurched at all the blood, dried now in his hair and on his shirt. He'd sent her into the office to rent the room, as he'd ducked out of sight in the vehicle they'd picked up along the road. They'd stopped at a convenience store so she could buy painkillers for his head. He'd taken several dry, probably more than he should have.

"Ty, are you all right?" she asked.

He shook his head.

"Then let me take you to the E.R."

But Ty had pointed out that not only would a doctor see him, but the police would come, too, taking them both away. Locking them up. Him behind bars, her back in the psychiatric ward.

For him she'd risk her freedom, even her sanity. "You lost so much blood…."

He shook his head again. "I'm all right. Head wounds bleed a lot."

He would know.

"I don't need a doctor, Irina," he said, his dark blue eyes gleaming. From the pain or all the pain-killers he'd taken? "I just need you."

The admission cost him. She knew he'd struggled long and hard to need no one. He straightened away from the counter and pulled her into his arms. When he kissed her, she tasted resentment. He hated that he needed her, but he couldn't deny that need.

Any more than she could.

Clothes dropped with the same abandon of the night before, and once again they stepped, naked together, under a shower spray. Instead of soot running down his face from his hair, blood ran. The drain in the old motel clogged, and the water in which they stood turned red, bathing them in blood. Irina ripped the paper off the bar of soap and lathered it up, washing the blood from Ty's skin.

As she'd noticed before, he had so many scars. The circles of cigarette butts embedded into his skin, still apparent even all these years after his father died and the abuse ended. But the abuse hadn't ended. A ridge of flesh stood out on his left leg, an ugly scar not yet healed from when he'd fallen through the staircase trying to rescue Ariel. Another scar, only a little bit older, raised a ridge along his ribs. And now he bore new marks, red ones that would soon turn to bruises, from Roarke's fists and feet.

Her fingertips gentle, she rubbed the soapy lather over his scars and bruises. Muscles rippled beneath her touch, and a groan slipped out from between his gritted teeth.

"You're in pain!"

He shook his head, then pulled her closer. His erection, long, hard and throbbing, pressed against her hip, nudging her abdomen. "I'm hurting for you."

She could take his words literally. All his pain, all his recent injuries, were because he'd been trying to protect her, because of the curse. The never-ending vendetta. Would she and her sisters ever be safe? Were they safe now?

He sighed. "And you're just hurting…."

Tears stung her eyes, but she blinked them back. She couldn't fall apart again. She refused to relinquish the strength for which she'd fought so hard. "I wish I could hear them…."

"You will. They're fine," he insisted again.

And just as he did, blackness enveloped her. Bright stars, glittering bits of turquoise and pale blue ice, twinkled as if guiding her way.

I'm sure she's fine. David checked. There was no sign of her vehicle in the rubble. They're safe. Elena convincing herself.

Ty was hurt. Ariel's concern.

Now resentment flashed in Irina, the jealousy she couldn't help but feel over the closeness between Ty and her sister, but pure joy pushed it aside. She expelled a ragged breath of relief. "They're fine."

"You just heard them?" Hope lifted Ty's raspy voice as he repeated his question.

She threw her arms around him. Rejoicing or staking her claim? "Yes!"

"Your sisters? Both of them?"

She nodded, tears of relief and joy trickling out of her eyes, joining the water streaming from the shower nozzle over her head. "Yes."

Ty's crooked grin slid away as his jaw grew

rigid beneath his two-day beard. "But the guys?
You didn't hear them."

She reached up and pressed a kiss to his chin,
the soft hair tickling her lips into a smile. "They're
fine, too. Elena thought about David looking for
you. And Ariel's worried about you."

"You're sure—David's fine?" Relief sparkled in
Ty's eyes, gleaming in the navy-blue depths.

She nodded. "I've never heard his thoughts
but—"

His arms tightened around her. "That's good.
You don't want to be in David's head." *Any more
than mine.* A ragged breath slipped from his lips.
"They didn't get hurt."

She wasn't entirely sure no one had been hurt,
but they'd seemed more worried about her and Ty
than themselves. "They're fine."

For the moment. But once again she'd concentrate
on the moment and nothing else. Nothing but Ty.

He stood naked and glorious, the water running
over his hard-muscled body. Passion raised goose
bumps on her skin, and she shivered.

"You're cold," he said. "The water heater must
have run out. Let's get out of here."

"Not yet," she said, reaching for the soap again.
"I'm not done with you." She finished washing
him, sliding her soapy hands over every bit of his

skin while his did the same to her. Wet and slick, they stepped from the shower. Shivering again, with cold and anticipation, Irina reached for a towel.

But Ty already had one around her, rubbing the coarse terry cloth over her turgid nipples. Over the curls between her legs. Again and again with delicious friction. When her knees weakened and she nearly crumpled to the bathroom floor, he picked her up and carried her into the bedroom, laying her on the mattress and following her down with the hard, taut length of his body.

Their mouths met, clinging, savoring, mating with tongues and teeth. Breathing grew ragged and harsh even while their hands stayed gentle, stroking skin soft and damp yet from the shower.

Irina squirmed on the mattress, trying to part her thighs, trying to ask for more. But he made love to just her mouth. She shuddered, reaching a tiny climax just from the slide of his tongue between her lips. "Ty…"

His mouth slid from hers, nibbled along the edge of her jaw, then moved lower. He kissed her neck, the hollow beneath her ear, then nipped her lobe with his teeth, tugging gently. She bit her lower lip, holding in another cry of pleasure.

Embarrassed that it took so little for him to bring her to the edge of sanity.

His mouth moved lower, sucking at her pulse pounding at the base of her throat, beating madly for him. Just for him.

"Ty…" She twisted, reaching between them, trying to close her hand over his penis, which throbbed against her hip. She only managed to brush a finger over the engorged tip, swiping a drop of moisture, which she raised to her lips, tasting his pleasure.

He groaned and uttered her name as a warning. Maybe it didn't take much for her to bring him to the edge. She wanted to know. She reached down again, this time closing her fingers around his hard length. She stroked, but he shifted away, pulling free of her grasp.

Then his mouth moved lower on her, along the curve of her breasts, his tongue lapping her cleavage, then the hard tips. He nipped at her, tugging at her nipples until she came again, melting into the mattress, turning liquid beneath him. She rallied, though, finding strength to wrestle with him. To close her hand around him, to gently tug.

His blue eyes flared hot with desire as his control snapped. He parted her legs and drove into her, drove her up and out of her mind with pleasure as he thrust again and again. She wrapped her legs around his waist, hanging on for the ride as long as it lasted. When orgasm after orgasm shuddered through her, and he buried himself inside her with one last guttural groan and exploded with heat and passion, she still clung to him.

Unwilling to ever let him go…

As they lay together in the dark, wrapped tight in each other's arms as on that first night, their thoughts mirrored each other's. *This could be our last time.*

Roarke's eyes grew heavy as pain and frustration gnawed at his temples. Son of a bitch. Ty McIntyre had been so close to death. They all had.

The tires of his van strayed off the asphalt, hitting the loose gravel of the shoulder. He fought with the wheel, steering away from the deep ditch back toward the center of the highway, deserted but for his vehicle.

He'd almost had them. But he'd been forced to watch them, helpless to stop them, as they'd all escaped death yet again. The others had taken cover inside while the dark-haired witch had driven McIntyre to safety.

Anger surged through him, and he slammed his

fist into the steering wheel. Pain radiated from his
knuckles to his wrist, but it was nothing compared
to what throbbed in his head. He glanced in the
rearview mirror at the bruises forming on his neck,
the imprint of McIntyre's fingers. Like his head,
his throat throbbed.

McIntyre had almost killed him. The suspended
cop shouldn't have been that strong, shouldn't
have been stronger than him. Once Roarke had the
charms, *he* would be the most powerful.

The witches and their men wouldn't escape him
then. But first he had to get the charms.

McIntyre and the witch had lost him in the fog
that had rolled out after the explosion. There'd
been a lot of smoke and dust but not much else.
The parking structure hadn't crumbled. Maybe
he'd set something up wrong or the explosives
hadn't been as destructive as his friend had
claimed. That "friend" would soon learn the con-
sequences of crossing Donovan Roarke. He'd deal
with him after he'd dealt with the witches.

McIntyre had probably made another car
switch. Koster and Dolce had been careful to lose
his tail. But he didn't intend to follow them. He
already knew where they were going.

Because he followed *her.* The witch who led
him back to where she died. Her ghost shimmered

on the road ahead of him in a thick cloud of smoke like the one that had risen from the explosion of the parking garage. His anger eased. It was probably better that the explosion hadn't been worse. He hadn't intended for the witches to die from the bomb, just their men—those besotted fools who'd lay down their lives for the witches.

They hadn't yet, but they would. Roarke intended to kill them every bit as painfully as he would the witches, as he had *her*.

She beckoned to him, glowing as if lit from within with flames. He'd lit her from the outside, the way he would light them. All of them.

And he would make damned sure McIntyre didn't escape this fire. As he watched the witch in the road ahead, the image changed. He was the one on fire, the robed figures encircling him. Not just the three witches but also their three men. Like the cult he'd formed to vanquish witches, they had formed one to vanquish him.

"No!" he shouted, blinking the image away. They'd frustrated him at every turn, always staying one step ahead of him. But not now.

When they got to Armaya, he would already be there. Ready for them.

Chapter 12

"Let me drive," Irina said.

But as before, Ty ignored the offer as he tried to ignore the pounding in his head and at the base of his skull. If Roarke lived with this kind of pain because of his brain tumor, Ty could almost understand his madness.

Irina slapped his shoulder in reprimand. "You're sympathizing with the devil. I knew you needed your head examined last night."

"I prefer how we spent our evening." In each other's arms. For the last time? One way or another, they were going to end today. Once she was reunited with her sisters, she wouldn't need him.

And if Roarke showed up and he actually succeeded...

He shuddered, then he glanced toward the passenger seat. Had she heard his thoughts? She stared straight ahead, but she had that look he'd seen on her so many times before, that look that anyone meeting her for the first time would mistake for blindness. Her dark eyes glazed over, unseeing, and she focused entirely on what she heard...inside her head.

"Irina, what is it?" he asked.

She shook her head as if trying to dispel the thoughts, and her honey-toned skin paled to alabaster.

His heart beat faster; she had to be hearing Roarke. Nothing upset her like *his* thoughts. She drew her bottom lip between her teeth, biting it as if trying to hold in a cry. Of fear? Of pain?

Was she in Roarke's head or one of his victim's?

Last night her sisters and his friends had been okay. But there was always the possibility that Roarke had gotten one of them. In the past, he'd kidnapped Elena's daughter. Someone who would terrorize a four-year-old had no conscience, no soul. Ty knew that well.

Irina shifted against the seat, the worn vinyl crackling beneath her. Then she moaned.

"Irina, are you all right?" He gripped the wheel hard, about to pull off the road. To take her in his arms. But he couldn't protect her from her thoughts.

She nodded finally, a mere jerk of her chin. Her rich chocolate-colored curls tangled around her shoulders and the torn vinyl seat of the old beater Bronco he'd picked up cheap. He'd worried that the rusted-out SUV might not be able to make the trip up north.

But he turned to focus on the road and slowed for the city-limits sign of Armaya. They passed a short block of businesses, a diner, a hardware, an old five-and-dime as well as a couple of other establishments. There wasn't much to Armaya but the vendetta. Two women—Irina's aunts—had been brutally murdered just on the outskirts of town. If Ty believed what Irina did, three women had been murdered here.

Including her mother. Was that what she thought about—the horrible way her mother died? The same way Elena had seen her baby sister die in a vision.

He reached across the seat and found her hand, then entwined their fingers. Nothing would happen to her…while he was alive.

"We're almost there," he warned her as he pulled onto a rutted lane that would lead them toward a farm, abandoned but for the ghost Ariel had seen here. Encircling the farm and edging the road was a cornfield, the stalks stripped of ears and abandoned to dry in the autumn sun. "Actually we're already here."

Irina turned toward him, her dark eyes bright with fear and an eerie anticipation. "*He's* here, too."

Ty pulled up next to a black Escalade parked near the abandoned farmhouse. "So are David and Ariel." A black Navigator was parked on the other side of the Escalade, nearer the barn. Sunshine glinted off its windshield. "Joseph and Elena are here, too."

"And the little girl? My niece?"

"They wouldn't have brought Stacia." Every measure had been taken to ensure the little girl's safety. "They found her a nanny with a black belt and a marksmanship medal."

Her lips tipped up into a smile. "They're always prepared." Her smile slid away. "They won't be. They won't know that he's here. He beat us here, Ty."

"Shh…" He pulled her across the seat and into his arms, but he kept his gaze sharp, intent for any movement outside the Bronco. "They'll be prepared."

She squirmed, then held up her palm. The little crescent moon glowed in the morning light. Then clouds shifted, and the sky darkened as if it were nearly sunset instead of daybreak. And the moon glowed brighter in her hand, as if the charm had stolen the sunshine.

"The charm will keep you safe and remind you of who and what you are," Irina murmured, repeating the words Ty knew their mother had spoken to them, relaying the legend of their heritage and the vendetta, right before their family was torn apart, before their lives were torn apart.

They had all thought that Irina would have had the best life. She hadn't been forced to live with a crazy old woman who'd hated the half of her that was Cooper instead of McGregor. She hadn't been bounced from foster home to foster home because she'd seen ghosts. She had been adopted by a loving couple…who hadn't been able to love her at all.

"Will the charm be enough?" she asked, staring down at the little moon. "Will it be enough to protect us from what he has planned?"

He stared out at the farm, at the corn stalks wavering as the wind picked up. The clouds darkened more, and in the distance thunder rumbled. "It's going to be too wet for a fire," he observed.

Large raindrops splattered against the windshield. "Maybe we should stay inside and wait this out," he suggested as his gut tightened with nerves and that same strange anticipation he'd glimpsed in her eyes.

It was almost over. One way or another, the witch hunt would end soon.

Irina shook her head. "The others are out there, waiting for us."

And so was Roarke. Were his friends aware of the madman's presence? He hadn't parked his vehicle near theirs, but it was around here somewhere. Ty didn't need Irina's mind-reading ability to know that Roarke had beaten them to the spot where her mother died.

He was the only one who knew exactly where that was.

Irina pulled back from his arms, pocketed the charm and then reached for the door handle, correcting him, "*I* know where my mother died."

From past experience, Ty knew arguing with her was useless once her mind was made up. She wouldn't stay in the car, no matter that the thunder rolled closer and lightning broke jagged cracks in the dark sky.

"I have the charm," she said again, either to soothe his troubled thoughts or her own.

Ty stepped out of the Bronco, his foot slipping in the mud, jarring his bad leg. He slammed the door, but a clap of thunder swallowed the sound of metal slapping against metal. The clouds hung so low and dark, Ty bowed his shoulders as if passing through a too-short doorway. He joined Irina at her side of the SUV, where she stood, rain streaking her face as she gazed at the house and the field.

"Are you sure?" he asked. Not just about where her mother had died but about the rest of her plan. He'd tried arguing with her, but he'd never known anyone as stubborn as she was. Not even David.

"Yes, this way." She started toward the field behind the skeleton of a barn, so many boards missing that only the half-collapsed roof and posts stood yet.

Ty caught her around the shoulders, encircling them and pulling her close to his side so he could shield her. Then with his other hand he reached for the gun tucked into the waistband of his jeans. Roarke's Glock. When Irina had bought the pain-killers, he'd also had her pick up more ammunition for the gun.

As a condition of his suspension, he wasn't supposed to be carrying a weapon. Another bridge burned to his old life, his old career. None of that mattered; nothing mattered but keeping Irina safe.

"Do you remember any of this?" he asked her as they walked across the overgrown yard to where the field began. "From when you were little?" And not just from her mother's thoughts.

She nodded. "Some. The Bowerses didn't want me to remember any of my life before them."

So they had worked hard to eradicate her memories, to eradicate her identity. How could they not have appreciated the special girl she was? Even when he'd been half-dead in the hospital emergency room, he'd instinctively known how special she was.

"They tried to love me," she said, as she often had in their defense. Had she grown up feeling that way—as if no one could love her?

His arm tightened around her shoulders. "You're not hard to love."

God, he wished she were, though. He wished he didn't feel the way he did…because no matter what happened, he was going to have to let her go. He'd held on to her for far too long.

As they neared the edge of the cornfield, the rain beat down harder, pelting their shoulders and the backs of their necks as they bowed their heads. Water ran off the gun Ty held raised, his finger along the barrel—a cop's version of a safety so that he'd be ready when he needed to fire.

"Are you ready?" he asked Irina. Her hair hung in wet spirals around her shoulders, her sweater so saturated that it hung on her.

He wanted her out of harm's way, someplace safe. But until Roarke was caught or killed, there was no place safe for her…or her sisters.

He should have killed him yesterday, when he'd had the chance to strangle the life from Donovan Roarke with his bare hands. Had she stopped him, getting into his head the way she had so long ago? Or had his own conscience stopped him?

If he had a conscience, he didn't have to worry about becoming his father's son. All he had to worry about right now was keeping Irina alive.

She shrugged off his arm and pulled away from him. "I have to lead. I know where we're going." Then she ducked between the rows.

The wind picked up, bending the stalks so they slapped against their bodies as they moved through the field. Ty stayed close behind her, keeping up with her quick pace. The mud sucked at the soles of their shoes, straining Ty's aching leg with each step. He shoved aside the pain, determined to ignore it, and concentrated on the field, on every rustle of a stalk, every shift of the wind.

Lightning illuminated the dark sky. A few rows over, Ty spied a shadow, a glimpse of a brown robe. Roarke was close. But the clouds shifted, dropping lower, spreading darkness. And Ty couldn't discern what was shadow and what real. A mere fraction of the confusion Irina must have felt all those years, wondering if the voices she heard were real.

Each snap of a stalk had his head jerking around, trying to watch all the angles, to make sure Roarke didn't sneak up on them.

Irina strode ahead of him. If not for the mud sucking at her shoes, she would have been running.

"Are you sure you know where you're going?" he asked, yelling the question over the rumble of thunder.

He'd no more than asked the question when the rows opened to a clearing. Irina turned back to him, her dark eyes wide with fear and sadness, as if she were saying goodbye. Then she stepped from the rows into the clearing, leaving him behind.

Irina's heart beat fast, hammering against her ribs as she walked into the clearing to her sisters. They stood near a tall pole someone had erected in the middle of the cornfield, the wood scorched black. Despite the stormy autumn wind and the cleansing rain, the odor of smoke and gasoline hung yet in the air, acrid in her nostrils. The two women standing near the pole glanced up, their heads and bodies covered by brown hooded robes.

As in *his* thoughts. *His* fears. Just like she'd planned. Last night, after they'd made love, Ty had gone down to the pay phone. He'd called David and relayed *her* plan.

The women's lips lifted in wide smiles, and they held out their arms. She had been so wrong to put off seeing them. Their faces held no re-crimination, no disapproval. Only love.

For her.

Irina ran, sliding in the mud, nearly falling before reaching them, before hurling herself into their arms. Lightning crackled, the air alive with electrical charges. All she felt was the warmth of her big sisters' embraces.

"God, Irina, we've been so worried," Elena murmured as she clutched her little sister close.

"We've missed you so much," Ariel said, her voice choked with emotion. "We've been looking for you…for so long…."

Tears slid down Irina's face, joining the rain. Both her sisters cried, too, the way they'd wept that night, the night they'd been taken away from their mother. Right here in this clearing where their mother had parked the truck with the little camper on the back. The authorities had taken them away from *her* and each other twenty years ago.

Irina had been alone for so long. Until now…

No, until Ty.

She turned back toward where she'd left him, but she caught no glimpse of his black hair, no gleam of his eyes. He'd disappeared.

Wool scraped against her cheek as Ariel pulled a robe over Irina's shoulders, the hood over her head. As a raincoat, it wasn't effective. The wool sucked up the water, weighing down her limbs, laying a burden across her back. But then, the robes weren't about protection against the rain.

Ariel shuddered, her body trembling against Irina's. "This whole thing…"

It would work. It had to or they'd never be free of the curse and Donovan Roarke. Irina looked beyond her sisters to the pole, to the pile of ashes beneath it. The rain tried to pound them into the earth, but they stayed, white dust atop mud.

"She's here," Ariel murmured.

"Our mother? You see her ghost?" She knew that was Ariel's ability—from her thoughts and from Ty. But still she could see nothing but the sheets of rain as they slashed across the field with the lightning.

Ariel nodded, her turquoise eyes soft with

sadness and regret. "She's worried about us. She's so scared that he's going to hurt us…."

Elena reached for Irina again, her hands clutching at Irina's robe. "I know what his plan is. I had a vision about… I've seen what he intends to do." Fear pinched her face and haunted her pale eyes.

These were special women, her sisters. Strong women who knew fear but dealt with it, facing it head-on instead of hiding from it.

Irina lifted her chin. "I know."

Elena's pale eyes widened. "You've heard him…."

She nodded.

Ariel stared at something near the pole, something Irina couldn't see. "She says we'll be fine. As long as we stay together…and use the charms. Did you bring the charm?"

Irina nodded again, then turned toward the surrounding field. "He's here."

Even if she hadn't heard him, she would have felt him watching them. His eyes radiated the hatred burning in his heart. She braced herself as the wavering stalks parted and a man stepped from the field. He wore a robe like the ones they were wearing, like the ones David and Joseph were supposed to be wearing. But she knew it wasn't one of her sisters' men.

It was her mother's killer. He walked toward them, but as he neared, fear joined his hatred.

Just as she'd planned.

Then he reached under his robe, pulling out something metal with a cylinder attached to it. He pointed a wide nozzle at them where they stood together beside their mother's ashes. "Give me the charms," he ordered.

"We don't have them," Ariel said, her voice a melodious taunt. Despite her bravado, she trembled.

Irina's limbs trembled, as well, chilled to the bone beneath the saturated wool robe. This was it. As Ty had feared, the witch hunt would end today. One way or the other.

"Lying witch!" Roarke shouted at the redhead. "You have them. I can *feel* them."

So could Irina. Since her sisters' embrace, the charm's heat had intensified, spreading warmth from her pocket throughout her wet clothes.

"Give them to me!" he shouted. A clap of thunder echoed his demand.

"No!" all three sisters returned in perfect unison, as if rehearsed.

Roarke did something to the metal thing in his arms, and fire shot from the nozzle, spraying out at them like water. Despite the rain, flames raced from him to them, burning a trail across the scraggly weeds and mud. "Give them to me now or die like your mother."

He lifted the torch so the nozzle tipped up…directly at them. But before he could pull the trigger and shoot more flames, a dark figure erupted from the stalks, knocking him to the ground. The flamethrower fell from his hands, the nozzle embedded in the mud. The two figures—one in a robe, one without—grappled in the field.

Ty.

He was still too weak to fight. He'd lost so much blood from the head wound Roarke had inflicted during their last confrontation.

"Ty!" she screamed. And the fear she'd fought so hard to suppress raced through her.

Grunts and groans emanated from the men as they rolled around the muddy field, throwing fists and lifting knees. Irina's heart clenched as she reeled under the onslaught of Ty's pain. His head throbbed. His leg ached. Each blow Roarke landed weakened him more.

He had a gun. He had Roarke's gun. Why hadn't he shot Roarke? Why hadn't he killed him as they'd planned? Because he didn't want to be his father. He didn't want to be Roarke. He didn't want to be a killer, not even for her.

A shot rang out. But it was the robed figure who stood, brandishing a gun.

And the dark-haired man lay in the mud, rain washing blood from his face and chest.

Unconscious or dead?

Chapter 13

Her heart contracting with fear, Irina started toward Ty, but her sisters pulled her back as Roarke advanced on them. Two other men, clad in those brown robes, burst from the stalks. But they were too late. Roarke was too close, the gun trained on them.

One of the men, his hood falling back to reveal blond hair, knelt in the mud next to Ty's body. His hand first touched Ty's head, then his throat.

Feeling for a pulse?

Sobs rose in Irina's throat, choking her, but she swallowed them down. He had to be all right. He had to be. She hadn't planned *this*.

"Give me the charms," Roarke shouted, "and I might let them live."

Not the witches but the two men he knew stood behind him, helpless to do anything. Metal gleamed in both men's hands; they were armed. But if they shot, Roarke could go down firing and kill all three of the sisters.

Their thoughts flitted through Irina's head, their fear, their helplessness to protect the women they loved. She hadn't heard them before; she didn't know them, but they loved the same people she loved.

No thoughts from Ty reached her even though she closed her eyes and concentrated, desperate to connect with him as she once had so long ago. To bring him back from the brink of death. *Ty, don't leave me. I need you.*

Her sisters whispered, drawing her attention the way they had when she'd been alone in the alley. "Irina…"

She had to summon the strength she hadn't realized she'd possessed until she'd met Ty. She had to put aside her paralyzing fear for his safety and focus on Roarke. She couldn't help Ty unless she survived the witch hunt.

Unless she ended the witch hunt.

God, she hoped her mother was right; the thoughts of both the living and the dead woman.

"Give me the charms!" Roarke shouted, his voice vibrating with rage while his dark eyes gleamed with madness.

"Let's give him the charms," Irina agreed, drawing hers from her pocket as her sisters drew out theirs.

Roarke stepped closer. With the hand not holding the gun, he reached out. Instead of dropping the charms into his open palm, they joined their hands; they joined their charms. While the sky darkened more, turning black, light emanated like a beacon from their joined hands, from the charms they held. The light flashed like a strobe, growing more brilliant as it gained power, as they gained power.

From their lips sprang Latin words, phrases they hadn't even known they knew. The words their long-dead ancestor, the witch, had spoken when she'd healed Roarke's long-dead ancestor, the madman who had begun the witch hunt. But they reversed the words and the sentiment.

Roarke backed up, his eyes wide with fear. The gun dropped from his hand as he threw up his arms as if to fend them off. But he needn't have feared any external threat. His greatest threat had always been from within.

The men behind him started forward, toward him, then flinched and grimaced. David and Joseph shrank back. Their eyes widened in horror.

In the middle of the clearing, on the very spot where he'd burned their mother alive, Donovan Roarke burst into flames. His screams of agony short as the fire consumed his body, his bones dissolving into ashes.

Don't die on me. Don't you dare die on me. The words reverberated inside Ty's aching head.

God, the pain was too much. Leaving his eyes closed would be so much easier than fighting to awaken. As when he'd been a kid, he was exhausted from fighting.

Come on, Ty. I know you can hear me. Listen to me like you did before. Wake up.

That had been so long ago. A lifetime ago. So much had happened to him since. She'd happened to him. Again. But was she in his head or standing next to him, talking in his ear?

He had to know. His lids heavy, he struggled to lift them. When he'd managed a squint, he flinched against the light, the pain threatening to shatter his skull. Something started beeping, the pace quickening as he fought.

"Give him more morphine. The anesthesia wore off too soon. He's going to go into shock—"

His body shook violently, beyond his control, rattling the bed and the tubes and machines connected to him. Was he dying? He couldn't die. Not without telling Irina how he felt about her. But that wouldn't be fair; they had no future…because he had no future.

No job. Maybe no freedom.

Maybe no life…

Ty!

Irina's body reeled with his pain. She'd wanted into his head, wanted to make him fight the way she'd made him fight so long ago. But she'd not been prepared for his pain, for the agony that tore through his body.

"Irina, are you all right?" Elena asked as she slid her arm around her shoulders, still the protective older sister.

Irina shook her head. "Ty…"

"He'll be okay," David said, his deep voice vibrating with emotion as a muscle ticked in his rigidly held square jaw. Was he trying to convince himself as much as the others? "This is *Ty*. He's the strongest person I know. Nothing can keep him down. Not a broken bone. Not a bullet to the brain."

Ariel wound her arms tighter around her fiancé, holding him, offering him the comfort Irina longed to offer Ty. Joseph Dolce sat behind his fiancée, tall and dark to Elena's small and pale. His fingers drummed the stiff back of the waiting room couch. He uttered no words of support, his eyes dark with concern and resignation.

He thought Ty was going to die—she didn't have to read his mind to know that. But he didn't know Ty the way David did. Neither did the surgeon who'd come into the waiting room a little while ago to tell them he'd removed the bullet; he didn't believe it had done any permanent damage. He couldn't believe it had entered Ty's skull on the angle it had and not killed him instantly. But the swelling and blood loss might kill him yet. Irina had read his mind; she knew that, although he offered them hope, he doubted Ty would ever regain consciousness.

"I'm sorry," she whispered to the blond man who was tortured with concern for his best friend.

He shook his head, refusing to accept her apology or her blame. "It wasn't your fault, Irina."

"It was *my* plan," she reminded him, as misery pooled in her stomach, rising to strangle her. "I thought it would work…."

"It did work," Elena reminded her, then shuddered. And Joseph's arm slipped from the back of the couch to encircle her slim shoulders. "Donovan Roarke is dead."

"Not that anyone will believe us," Ariel said. "I can't believe what happened…."

"They can do DNA on the ashes, confirm it's him," David said as he pushed a slightly shaking hand through his hair, tousling the blond tresses.

"How can they confirm we didn't kill him?" Joseph asked.

But they had. Just as Irina had planned. Ty thought himself a killer, but she was more like Roarke, more like Ty's father, than he was. Poor Ty….

David shrugged. "I'm not sure what happened. Maybe his flamethrower malfunctioned. He probably had gas on his clothes."

The blowtorch hadn't been anywhere near where he died, next to the pole to which he'd tied their mother, where his ashes had joined hers.

"Maybe we can say it was lightning," Joseph offered. They all knew it wasn't. It had been the power of the three charms combined, protecting them as their mother had foretold.

Had they protected Ty? While they'd waited for the ambulance, the three sisters had knelt beside him in the mud. They'd joined their hands and their charms, pressing them to his heart, willing him to live. The light had glowed again, bright as the sun within their grasp.

But Ty hadn't opened his eyes. He hadn't even stopped bleeding. He'd lost so much blood....

Please, Ty, come back to me....

"How will we prove Donovan Roarke murdered our mother?" Elena asked, either unaware of Irina's inner turmoil or trying to distract her. "And our aunts. And all the others…"

Like the Bowerses, whom Irina was suspected of murdering. Going to jail or an asylum was the least of her concerns.

"He kept a journal, like Eli McGregor had," David said. "Joseph and I found his car in the cornfield. That was why we were late…."

Too late to stop Ty from putting himself in danger.

David had had other security guards in the field, clad in the brown robes, to protect the sisters. But with everyone wearing the same thing, Roarke had been able to get close to them. Almost close enough to burn them alive.

"Everything's in that journal," Joseph shared. "We turned it over to the police."

So much of the last few hours was a blur for Irina, like much of her past. She remembered her and her sisters joining the charms over Ty. Then police officers and paramedics had arrived, but she didn't remember them. She didn't remember getting to the first hospital or the helicopter airlifting Ty back here, to Barrett. Had she ridden in the helicopter, too?

She remembered nothing but Ty lying in that muddy cornfield in Armaya, bleeding to death. Because of her.

Why hadn't he shot Roarke? Was it because of the robes—because he hadn't been sure who'd been walking toward her and her sisters? He wouldn't have taken the chance of killing an innocent man. The robes had been her idea, to scare Roarke. So it was Irina's fault that Ty hadn't been able to save himself.

Ty, come back to me. Fight for your life. Fight for us.

Or didn't he believe he had anything to fight for? She'd never told him she loved him.

"Can the journal be used to get Ty out of trouble for what he did for me?" Irina asked, guilt and gratitude warring within her. She loved Ty for being the man he was, her rescuer, but she wished she hadn't had to be rescued. That she would have been strong enough to take care of herself.

David nodded. "I'll make damned sure it is. I'll

talk to the police commissioner, the mayor—hell, the governor if I have to."

Irina's lips lifted into a small smile at Ty's friend's loyalty. She'd worried that she'd caused trouble between them, that she might have cost Ty his friends as well as his job. But she needn't have worried. Not everyone in life was like the Bowerses; they could love someone who didn't always do what they wanted.

And if Ty's friends were like that, was he? Could he love her no matter what? Could he *love?*

She knew he was determined not to, that he worried about being like his father, about continuing the cycle of abuse. But he wouldn't. He wasn't capable of hurting anyone...except to defend himself or someone else.

She should have told him how she felt, should have said the words aloud. Now she could only say them in her head. *I love you. I love you. Please come back to me.*

The door to the waiting room opened again. A nurse in scrubs stepped inside. "Family of Tyler McIntyre?"

"Here," David answered, not bothering to explain they were friends instead.

Or were they such close friends they'd become family? Irina didn't feel as close to her sisters as she did to Ty, her bond to him deeper even than blood.

"He's awake," the nurse said, shock evident in her voice and widened eyes.

"Yes!" David shouted as if he'd won a personal victory. Ariel, Elena and Joseph echoed his sentiments in shouts of their own.

Irina said nothing as relief and emotion welled up and choked her. Tears gathered in her eyes, but she blinked them back. She didn't want to fall apart before she went in to see him.

"He's really weak, so we'll have to limit his visitors," the nurse said as everyone rushed forward. "Right now he's asking for only one person."

Irina rose, her legs trembling with reaction and nerves.

"David," the nurse finished.

The blond man cast an apologetic glance at Irina before following the nurse from the room. Elena's arm came around her shoulders again. "I'm sorry, honey…."

Me, too. Sorry she hadn't told him how she felt. When she'd seen him lying in the field, she'd thought it too late. But maybe that moment had passed even before then. Maybe there was no sense in loving a man who didn't want the responsibility of being loved, who couldn't love in return.

"I need a moment alone," she murmured as she pulled from her sister's embrace and walked from the room. Just a couple doors down the hall, she found the chapel, bathed in myriad colors from the sun shining through the stained glass window. The storm was over—or maybe it had been isolated to just that cornfield in Armaya.

After David had had Ty airlifted back to Barrett from the small county hospital just outside Armaya, he'd flown a leading neurologist in from Chicago. He'd spared no expense for his friend's life.

All Irina had done was try to slip inside his head. She had nothing to offer him but her love, which he didn't want. She reached into her pocket and pulled out the little crescent charm. She'd seen the evidence of its power in Roarke's demise; it had kept her and her sisters safe. Had it done the same for Ty? Is that how he'd recovered? Or had he heard her? Did he know how she felt about him?

"He says *you* can tell him," David said from where he leaned against the arched door frame.

Startled, Irina knocked her knee and her elbow against the pew. "You didn't—"

"Read your mind?" David asked, with a teasing grin. She could understand now why Ariel loved him so much. "No. But *he* did. He says for you to get out of his head—"

And out of his life? Fear gripped her heart.

"And into his room," David finished.

Relief flooded her, and she jumped up to follow David to the automatic doors of the ICU. Before she could walk to the bed where Ty lay, connected to machines, David caught her hand.

He squeezed her fingers, then warned her, "Don't hurt him."

The threat was fair. She didn't have a great track record with regard to not hurting those she cared about. The Bowerses were dead, her roommate and probably the only real friend she'd had was missing. And Ty lay here, in the Intensive Care Unit….

Legs leaden now, she walked slowly through the doors to stand beside Ty's bed. Maybe he'd be safer if she didn't care about him, if she just walked away.

"You're not going anywhere," Ty told her as he turned his bandaged head toward her. His blue eyes gleamed bright with amusement and…

Dare she think it?

"Love," he answered her thought.

He had gotten inside her head, too. He could read her thoughts. "Ty…"

"Are you all right?" he asked her even though he was the one who'd just had a bullet removed from his brain.

She nodded. "Roarke's dead."

"I know. David told me."

Was that why he'd called his friend in first—to spare her the ordeal of recounting what had happened?

"I killed him," she said, staring down at the charm she hadn't realized she still held.

"No, you didn't. The charms did, whatever power you all have…"

"Witchcraft," she told him, half-amused.

All the stuff might have been in her apartment, but she'd never practiced. She'd never admitted who she was. But then how could she have admitted what she hadn't really known?

"For so long I hadn't known who I was," she shared with him. "There are still pieces of my life missing, probably because of the drugs or the alcohol. I haven't lived a pretty life, Ty."

"Neither have I," he said. "But all that's behind us, Irina. All the pain, it's over."

The doctors might argue that with him, but she wouldn't. She couldn't argue with a man who would always know what she was thinking.

"At least I won't feel any more pain, as long as

you say yes," he continued, then he lifted his hand. Lying in his palm like she held the charm was a diamond ring. The marquis stone twinkled in the fluorescent lights. This was why he'd called David in first, to get him a ring like he'd gotten him a neurologist.

The ring couldn't be for her. He'd been determined to never love anyone, to never need anyone…

"Marry me, Irina." He didn't ask. He didn't need to; he already knew what she was thinking, what she was feeling.

But sometimes a woman still needed to hear the words.

"I love you," he said.

Her heart expanded, filling with the love it had been deprived of for so long. Sometimes a woman needed to say the words, too. "I love you, Ty. I love you so much."

"This isn't just out of gratitude," he said as he slid the ring on her finger.

"No, my love for you is real. It has nothing to do with all the times you've saved my life." He would always be her hero, though, even when they were eighty and rocking their grandbabies.

He shook his head, then flinched as the bandages rustled against the pillow.

"Shh…" she said, pushing him back on the

pillow, unable to stop touching him, to stop reassuring herself that he was real. That he hadn't died in the clearing of that cornfield in Armaya.

"No, I'm talking about my gratitude to you," he corrected her.

As he did so often, she lifted a brow in question. "I don't understand…."

What had she brought to his life but pain and danger…and love?

"You saved my life. Twenty years ago," he reminded her. "And again today."

He reached up, touching her cheek with one hand while he grasped her fingers with the other. "You make my life worth living."

She'd brought him back to life, as he'd brought her. Now they would spend the rest of their lives together.

Epilogue

The bride stood before the long oval mirror, adjusting her veil. She turned back to her sisters, both clad in brilliant blue bridesmaid dresses. "Do I look all right? Something's missing."

"You look beautiful," Irina said, her heart full as she stood behind Ariel, staring over her shoulder in the mirror. "Absolutely breathtaking…"

"Says the woman who did the quickie Vegas wedding," griped Elena with a delicate snort of disgust. She sat by the vanity, winding flowers as well as sprigs of lavender and sandalwood into her daughter's blond curls.

Irina giggled, still amused by her sisters' disdain for her ceremony. She and Ty had had so little fun in their lives that they'd enjoyed every minute of their wedding, officiated by none other than Elvis. Ty, even with his head still shaved from his surgery, had looked dashing in a borrowed tuxedo. And Irina had worn a gown, although not as elaborate as Ariel's Cinderella gown with the sweetheart neckline. She'd looked more like a flapper in her fringed white dress.

"I know what it needs," Ariel muttered, running her fingertips along the lace edging of her neckline. "Mama's locket."

Irina shuddered, remembering the soot embedded under her sisters' nails after they'd dug through their mother's ashes, looking for the locket. They'd returned to Armaya, and in the middle of the cornfield they'd erected a monument to their mother, to where she'd died her agonizing death. Finally her ghost had found peace; she didn't appear to Ariel anymore, although Irina knew her sister would have loved seeing her mother today, on her wedding day. Or at least having a part of her with her, with them.

"I'm sorry we couldn't find it," Elena said. They'd searched through all of Donovan Roarke's things as well as their mother's ashes.

The locket had belonged to a McGregor, having

been the only thing to survive the fire that had killed the female members of the McGregor family. Eli McGregor's son had given it to Myra Durikken's daughter, betraying his father by letting the girl go so she wouldn't be burned alive like her mother.

Elena Durikken had brought the locket to America with her, along with the charms. Since her mother had given the locket to her, Myra Cooper had always worn it. She'd given her daughters the charms but not the necklace.

Or had she?

Hands shaking, Irina opened the closet and reached for the box she stored in this room, a spare guest room in Ty's new house. He'd sold all the properties he'd owned, some of them being valuable commercial land, and after investing most of the money, he'd bought this gorgeous estate he and Irina shared. David and Ariel were to be married in the garden; outside, an orchestra played for the guests gathering on the estate for the wedding.

"Aunt Irina, what are you looking for?" Stacia asked as Irina dragged down the cumbersome box.

"A picture, sweetie," she explained to the niece she already loved so much her chest hurt.

"You shouldn't be reaching like that," Elena tsked, probably fearing for the bodice of Irina's bridesmaid dress—or the waistline.

"I've got it," she said. She'd cleaned out the apartment she'd shared with her missing room-mate but kept this box of Maria's things. From it she pulled a picture of her and her roommate, the twenty-year-old who looked so much like Irina with her big Gypsy eyes and long curly hair. They could have been twins instead of friends—or, at the very least, sisters.

Irina pressed her fingers to the photo, to the antique locket that had always hung around Maria's neck. "Oh my God…"

"We have another sister," Elena murmured as she stared over Irina's shoulder.

Irina stroked her finger over her younger sister's face. "Maria."

"Mother was pregnant when she lost us," Elena realized. "She'd worn all those loose gowns. I'd just thought she'd gotten heavy."

"With child." As Irina was now, with Ty's baby. She took one hand from the picture to rub over her distended abdomen.

"Maria," Ariel repeated the name as she, too, studied the photograph. "Where is she?"

"Running. Scared." Now Irina knew to whom some of the other thoughts she'd had in the alley belonged. Maria.

"We'll find her," Ariel said.

Irina nodded, a smile of pride tipping up her lips. "*Ty* will find her."

Her husband had begun his second career as a private investigator. The police department had offered his job back, but he'd wanted to work for himself. He'd wanted to help people find missing loved ones, like the sisters who had missed each other for so long. He was gaining worldwide recognition for the cases he'd already solved—her smile grew—with a little help from a trio of witches.

Although she didn't walk to the window, she knew where he stood, on the lawn below, waiting for her. His love enveloped her. Her and their unborn child.

She remembered her mother's hope for her children. That day she'd lost her daughters she had wished they would one day know a deep and enduring love.

Three of her daughters had found that love. They'd reunited with their charms. They were together and safe.

Ariel and Elena smiled, too. "We'll find Maria," they agreed. "And we'll convince her that she's safe, too, that the witch hunt is over."

* * * * *

Don't miss Death Calls, *the first story in Caridad Piñeiro's* THE CALLING *trilogy, available in the* NOCTURNE *mini-series in November 2008.*

*Mills & Boon® Intrigue
brings you a sneak preview of…*

Karen Whiddon's Bulletproof Marriage.

*After two years of thinking her Lazlo Group
spy husband Sean McGregor is dead, SIS agent
Natalie Major is stunned when she calls for
help from a mission gone bad – she's trapped
by enemy fire – and out of the smoking ruins
her husband strides towards her, back from the
dead…to avenge his own "murder" and to
win back the woman he loves!*

Don't miss this thrilling new story in the
MISSION: IMPASSIONED *series, available
next month in Mills & Boon® Intrigue!*

Bulletproof Marriage

by

Karen Whiddon

If reinforcements didn't show up soon, Natalie Major thought grimly, she might as well paint a target on her chest and leap into the open. The unknown assassin—or assassins—were that close. The decaying concrete warehouse she'd holed up in only had two ways out—and one of them had been blown to rubble.

She needed help. Corbett Lazlo, her father's oldest friend and owner of one of the top private investigative agencies in the world, had promised to send someone. She'd asked for the best.

Now she wished she'd asked for the most prompt.

Gallows humor. She'd never been particularly good at it before, though she'd grown more proficient.

Her husband wouldn't even recognize her now if he were still alive. Once, he'd been Lazlo's top agent. She'd married a Lazlo Group spook, just like her own father had been. Retired now, and in a wheelchair, her father lived in relative seclusion. Her beloved husband, Sean, hadn't been so lucky. He'd been killed two years ago this week. Lazlo's group seemed to be the ruin of everyone she loved, so in honor of her dead husband and disabled father, and in defiance of the Lazlo legacy she could easily have embraced, she'd worked her way to the top of SIS, the British Secret Intelligence Service. There was no job too difficult, no task too dangerous for Sean McGregor's widow.

Until now.

She scouted the area. Trapped inside the abandoned warehouse, she was fast running out of options. The concrete walls made a good shield against bullets, but she needed to see her enemies. Right now, she could only hear them. And it was hard to fight when you had no idea who the enemy might be. Or where they were hiding.

Plus, cement was cold and hard and reminded her too damn much of a tomb.

The shooters fired off another round of shots. AK-47s. Random bullets ricocheted crazily and dangerously off the cement walls and floors. She couldn't even dodge them, having no idea where they'd go.

She'd found the abandoned warehouse two days

ago. A concrete bunker in a run-down area of Glasgow had seemed relatively safe. Not wanting to endanger others by staying at a B and B or hotel, she'd used the concrete warehouse as her base, returning to sleep and regroup while attempting to gather information on whoever had sold out her team. Since Millaflora—a low-down, no-good mole operating as a double agent inside the SIS—had already been caught, she had no idea who she was looking for.

Officially, she was on administrative leave, supposedly holed up, incognito in an unknown luxury hotel on the French Riviera. No one in her office knew she'd come to Glasgow, not even her supervisor.

And though she'd tried to take extraordinary precautions similar to those she used when deep undercover, her enemy had found her.

Whoever "they" were.

She supposed the whys and the hows didn't matter. Not now. All that mattered was that if help didn't arrive soon, she was dead.

Her ammo nearly gone, no backup, and no alternative plan—pretty shoddy situation for an undercover agent who'd recently been promoted to team leader.

It had to have something to do with the code. Natalie was sure of it. She'd been so close to cracking it. She and her team.

Now they all were dead and she was on the run.

And she had only herself to rely on. In seven years of service, she'd never had a single casualty. Until now. Now she'd lost her entire team. They'd been eliminated, killed in a way that left no doubt she was next. All the codes they'd been working on had disappeared, at least as far as anyone knew. She'd told no one that she'd made her own private copy.

Not knowing who was on her side, she hadn't dared to contact SIS. She'd called her father, knowing he'd contact Corbett, knowing Lazlo would help.

"Come on, reinforcements," she muttered. Her father'd told her Corbett had promised to send help. The head of the Lazlo Group never went back on his word.

A movement across the alley caught her attention. Finally! Someone had arrived to help her out of this hellhole.

She took another look and blinked, wondering if the stress had finally claimed her mind.

Out of the mist and smoke, a dead man strode toward her, keeping close to the wall, staying in the shadows, but coming. For her.

Natalie began to shake.

Shots rang out. Crouching, the man began to run. More shots. So far, he hadn't been hit. He'd always been lucky that way.

At least, until the day he'd died.

Dead. He was dead and buried.

Rocking back onto her heels, she rubbed her eyes and took another look.

She hadn't been wrong. The man she'd loved more than any other, her soul mate, her husband, the man she'd mourned, the man she'd never thought to see again, kept moving toward her.

Frozen, she watched as he continued, his low crouch purposeful and unafraid. Or maybe he didn't care. After all, a man couldn't die twice, right?

Her heart drummed in her ears. Sean. Her husband, Sean. This couldn't be real, couldn't be happening.

She wasn't the type to faint—not anymore. Too many hard lessons learned. Instead, she'd taught herself to push back, to fight.

But how did one battle a ghost?

From the smoke and the grave, against the periodic bursts of gunfire, he continued to come toward her. He moved exactly the way she remembered—purposeful and bold, dodging bullets as though he were untouchable. She'd often thought that very arrogance had been what had gotten him killed.

Killed.

Yet here he was, ducking under the concrete overhang into her shadowed hiding place, solid and real and alive.

When he reached her, he stopped, his dark gaze intense. She couldn't move. He was still beautiful, even in the dust and the dirt and the danger. She caught her breath, unable to speak.

"I'm here," he said, his voice husky, as though too long unused, a hint of wariness in his gaze.

"I…" She moved toward him, inspecting him, still unable to believe what the fates had just returned to her.

"Get down," he snarled, yanking her behind the concrete wall with him as the shooters let loose with several rounds of shots.

"What the—" he cursed, letting her go. "They've got AK-47s. You must have royally pissed someone off. Why are they trying to kill you?"

She still couldn't find her voice. Unable to help herself, she let her gaze roam hungrily over his muscular body—the way her hands used to.

"Either I'm dead, dying or you're not dead," she said, feeling like an idiot, still not sure what to think.

"No." His dark gaze locked with hers, daring her wrath. "I'm not dead."

Celebrate 100 years of pure reading pleasure with Mills & Boon®

To mark our centenary, each month we're publishing a special 100th Birthday Edition. These celebratory editions are packed with extra features and include a FREE bonus story.

Plus, you have the chance to enter a fabulous monthly prize draw. See 100th Birthday Edition books for details.

Now that's worth celebrating!

September 2008

Crazy about her Spanish Boss by Rebecca Winters
Includes FREE bonus story
Rafael's Convenient Proposal

November 2008

**The Rancher's Christmas Baby
by Cathy Gillen Thacker**
Includes FREE bonus story *Baby's First Christmas*

December 2008

One Magical Christmas by Carol Marinelli
Includes FREE bonus story *Emergency at Bayside*

Look for Mills & Boon® 100th Birthday Editions at your favourite bookseller or visit
www.millsandboon.co.uk

4 FREE

BOOKS AND A SURPRISE GIFT!

We would like to take this opportunity to thank you for reading this Mills & Boon® book by offering you the chance to take FOUR more specially selected titles from the Intrigue series absolutely FREE! We're also making this offer to introduce you to the benefits of the Mills & Boon® Book Club—

- ★ **FREE home delivery**
- ★ **FREE gifts and competitions**
- ★ **FREE monthly Newsletter**
- ★ **Exclusive Mills & Boon® Book Club offers**
- ★ **Books available before they're in the shops**

Accepting these FREE books and gift places you under no obligation to buy, you may cancel at any time, even after receiving your free shipment. Simply complete your details below and return the entire page to the address below. You don't even need a stamp!

YES! Please send me 4 free Intrigue books and a surprise gift. I understand that unless you hear from me, I will receive 6 superb new titles every month for just £3.15 each, postage and packing free. I am under no obligation to purchase any books and may cancel my subscription at any time. The free books and gift will be mine to keep in any case.

18ZED

Ms/Mrs/Miss/Mr ....Initials ....

BLOCK CAPITALS PLEASE

Surname ....

Address ....

....

....Postcode.................................

Send this whole page to:
UK: FREEPOST CN81, Croydon, CR9 3WZ